T0063124

Ashley and Her Mystical Tale

Bhavna Khemlani

PARTRIDGE

ISBN: Hardcover 978-1-4828-2661-6
Softcover 978-1-4828-2660-9
eBook 978-1-4828-2662-3



**To order additional copies of this book, contact**
Toll Free 800 101 2657 (Singapore)
Toll Free 1 800 81 7340 (Malaysia)
orders.singapore@partridgepublishing.com

www.partridgepublishing.com/singapore

A young teacher accepts a job at a strange school where nothing is as it seems. She must use every one of her abilities to unravel a supernatural mystery encountering a new taste of devotion and benevolence.

I dedicate this book to a passionate life.

Welcome to the school,

You are requested to join a new class. Dispose those expectations and simply take your seat before the bell rings and you miss the attendance to visualize and experience an enthralling connection with your new classmates.

With research and observations of surroundings, this story has been created. References to actual places or people are inspirational and fictitious.

The protagonists of this tale, Ashley Preston, Dominic Thurston, Edwin Brown and the students Jude Gilliam, Margarita Flinghead, Sarah Compton, Thomas Boyle, Viera Katz, Roy Demir, Edward Foreman, and Judy Lee will indisputably rekindle the forgotten and ignorant angst to those affiliations that ought to be chucked out, so one can savior the beat of a genuine existence.

The mystical personalities John Mosaic and Barney Peacock grace their magic with their unique powers.

In other words, Ashley is waiting to share her new journey into teaching at a new school which is no less than a treasure hunt.

The output of the journey certifies guaranteed investment of facts that are unified and needed in *The Classroom* which proposes an everlasting smile, thrill, obsession, and aspiration to never leave the school.

This story ensures the present to be a jackpot and a ticket to a future enterprise of zeal and chirpiness with no age barrier. Sip the moments in life and the days slipping by with enthusiasm and an upbeat zest.

The bell has rung!

Bhavna Khemlani

## CHAPTER 1

# Chapter Closed

The work of expectation is killing me. I can't stop thinking how is love beautiful for everyone? Is love even beautiful? Why do people have to even think of getting married? How I wish I could burp on this notion! There is already so much to do in one's life. Globalization is a bag full with wonderful activities, services, and of course unwanted drama. 'Why on earth does a woman even dream of a husband? What crap?' I say out loud.

The world of me—*Ashley Preston* has suddenly become a question mark. The obvious has become blurry and the blurry has become the obvious.

A break up was blurry and love was obvious. Now it has switched places to honor and soothe the comfort zone of Mr. Ego!

I am simply disgusted with the fact this had to happen. But it simply did. I took out my engagement ring and threw it in the oval shaped trashcan. The simply designed trashcan seemed way trustworthy than my ex—Edwin!

The ring was lying on layers of crumpled tissue papers that were used to absorb my grief and now the ring was shining on the accumulated despair I was attempting to throw away.

I could sense that it was simply glaring back at me with pity and its dull shine was trying to raise a toast to humility which simply got me quite furious. 'Stop staring at me you demented piece of rock!' Saying that out loud gave a sign of relief I hoped. In other words, it was better to gear up some energy and pack my labor of love back into another closet.

I went back into my so called room and started packing up all my stuff. It felt as if the demons had released me from a cage of struggle directing me to a new pathway of a magical spell.

Being born and brought up in Hawaii has always been heaven to me. I never thought of shifting elsewhere. I was told I have always been kind-hearted, ambitious and intelligent. Being a thirty-two year old museum curator and quitting to settling down with my ex-fiancé was huge for me. My practice was driven by curiosity, longing, and questions of cultural identity. Until one day when the arms of passion embraced every beat of my heart.

My ex fiancé—Edwin really meant to me and screwed up my life pattern with his kiss parade. While packing my skirts back into the maroon colored luggage, I could remember what a charmer he was. We met randomly in a sports club where I went regularly.

He was working as an accountant for a law firm. His smile could make any woman feel stimulated with a bright impact leaving a tickly feeling in the tummy.

Coincidently we met at random timings and eventually a smile, then a greeting, and a phrase was exchanged leaving us with an option to go on a date.

The thirty-five old, gray-green eyed man definitely got me into a hot soup for he was irresistible, flexible, a good listener, and of course loved me. We started to date and everything changed when he proposed.

I did many things I thought of rarely doing from bungee jumping, canoeing, eating frogs, watching opera, and walking over crushed glass pieces to mixing ketchup in vanilla ice cream. I think it was all bizarre and unbelievable.

How wonderful everything seemed? It looked superficial and dreamy. What happens when your fiancé feels the itch and is uncontrollable that can't differentiate between his fiancé and another woman? This happened twice.

God knows what happened to the mind of the accountant. His wisdom must have been caught up with the overflow of numbers. His flexibility seemed to be too stretchy to offer a pleasure of smooch to anyone he felt the need to express empathy.

I was forgiving enough to let go off a mistake I thought that had been done unintentionally; but not when he was seen kissing his colleague on her lips.

When I asked curiously, 'What was that, Edwin?' Very politely or let's say with a defensive manner he mentioned, "A goodbye kiss. What else would it be?"

His explanation about his colleague shifting back to Washington with her family was ridiculous. So to convey empathy and express his friendship, he had smooch his colleague leaving a trace of a lusty act. I knew it! Something seemed fishy.

But to my surprise, she was astonished and took it as a funny gesticulation leaving a wink as the cherry on top.

Knowing that I disliked it, he was again using his old tactics of reneging and started a new negotiation. I wanted to stick his lips on Mount Everest. My emotions were churning in my stomach then slowly rising up to my bosom. I was stunned to see how he actually was.

The fluctuation and the change in his compassion were now in disguise I presumed. I began to see his hidden mannerisms, gestures and the will to convey how he cares by kissing unnecessarily. He just never admitted he was wrong. A series of debate was echoing in my mind. When I spoke to him about it, he was furious and remembering how he began throwing his things insanely.

I even explained to him that I respected his privacy and friendship but if we were already dating, then engaged, it was not fine to kiss other women whatsoever.

The first year of dating was perfect, unusual and adventurous. The second year felt like I was walking down a hill where I started to only see him kissing other women. It seemed I was part of a kiss parade, I believed. I could not simply understand his craving. After convincing him for hours, he went to see a psychiatrist. But nothing seemed to change his domineering thoughts.

I was too busy with my life that I could hardly believe I could fall in love with anyone. I did worry about my workaholic attitude. I found falling in love the most time consuming piece of shit in this world where a chain of activities and emotions strangle a person leaving a choking sensation. My memories to great moments were diminishing to the rising dominance of pragmatic decisions.

This whole thing had messed my ambition as a Museum curator. As the head curator, I had the pleasure to supervise collections, such as artwork and historic items, and conducted public service activities at schools and universities. The Museum technicians and conservators organized and reinstated objects and documents in museum collections and displays. My career was surely at stake and I was worried with concern.

Now it seemed like I was a curator of my emotions that needed to be restored and be saved from submerging into the graveyard of misery.

I could see my suitcases sit down on the creamy white marble flooring. How peaceful they looked patiently waiting to be carried to their next destination. They seemed to be very excited and extremely elated to be traveling around while I was to organize yet another event of surviving a chapter to be closed.

As tears were trickling down my cheeks, I remember that I had decided after dating for a year this could have finally been the time where I could fulfill my maternal feeling. I was so happy to settle down with a man whom I fell in love with. Everything seemed perfect like every love story does. Until . . . it was crushed and evaporated like it meant nothing.

I manage to get up, take my luggage and leave. The flashback where Edwin had proposed to me and moving in with him got me feeling edgy. The thought to what we had decided to make our house a home became a preconceived notion. However, some kisses can create a chapter to close an entire relationship, I wonder with desolation.

I paused, took out my phone and texted Edwin:

*'Darling, your kiss parade has closed a chapter of love. And I have left the keys to soothe your ego until eternity. Never yours . . . A'*

I could no longer feel the need to stay in Hawaii even for a while. Days passed by, then weeks, all I felt was miserable and thought of the days where everything was normal. Work, friends, yoga and family were balanced. I needed no man. Sort of—I thought.

Dating once in a while was just a way to enjoy womanhood or some kind of a kinky act keeping the oestrogen full of life.

While placing my clothes back into my wardrobe, I could not believe that I remembered an argument I had with Edwin about children. Wheeling around, I took the red colored stool and sat on it.

He was having his breakfast and I was going through some pamphlets on donations posted to me. A fleeting thought on adoption came up and I turned to ask him randomly, 'A woman could adopt a child, right?'

"What happened suddenly? Hmm . . . adoption! I would love my own like any normal person, Ashley. But adopting is never too bad. A noble thought it is," said Edwin with displeasure.

'What would have happened if everyone had gotten married and no one adopted any children? The number of orphans would exceed bringing an emotional trauma to the world because of their depravity. Hmm . . . so this world should lean on people like us, I believe,' I replied with confidence.

"Why are you getting emo after seeing the pamphlets? Perhaps you can think of it later when the time is right. Don't get into a crappy mood, A," frowned Edwin.

'I am not in a crappy mood. But you speaking that way is trying to mess up with my pleasant mood. Anyway, I shall spend the day at the gym, spa and arranging more space for new furniture. You can have a great day—Mr. Not interested!' I said intentionally.

Oh, those days will soon feel like one of those days, I wondered.

After months of mourning to my love story, I finally decoded my mind to travel and live life. I started to surf on the internet for job opportunities worldwide. I had traveled to job fairs and sent my resumes to recruitment agencies. I was looking for something that would touch my soul making me feel alive again.

I have worked as a Museum curator for seven years. I had supervised and guided high school children during their visits for projects. Traveling with them to other museums, watching all sorts of videos from different cultures and even traveling to anthropological sites was nothing less than an adventure.

It had been two years being out of work and did not want to rust my abilities. I wanted to hunt for something new and better. So I visited the museum and coincidently bumped into some students who had visited the museum a few years ago and were already in college.

It was so admirable to see them grow and hatch out of their *'I am cool or you are a jerk attitude.'* I could see that sensibility does knock on everyone's door but not for some.

I had updated them about my exciting life and learnt one thing for sure. It is not time for me to make a home for myself.

But maybe make a thousand more homes for other children who needed a normal life.

My life is normal. Quite normal actually—it is more like I had to experience a blend of emotional sentiments in one go.

Now I feel I can fall in love again. This time it would be with my new work.

The students cheered for my comeback and their moral support was amicable.

## CHAPTER 2

# The Changing Fate

It was amazing to catch up with long lost people who had always been my well-wishers. It seemed just like waking up after a power nap. Like most women, I developed a bubble of hope that someday I shall adopt two children and have a happy family. That someday turned into a dooms day. I could feel my eyes teary with disappointment.

I decided to head home and see the bright side. While driving back, I realized I was one of the Americans that was never willing to live alone. I had set my boundaries and discussed about my privacy with my family. Even when I was completing my undergraduate studies, my parents were quite lenient and offered me a private phone line. I always loved living with them.

I appreciated my parents and tried not to skip the Sunday lunch or dinner we had together. That was the only way we could catch up. They are open-minded that I could introduce my friends, colleagues and dates to them. They have always understood and never tried to intrude in my life just because I was living with them.

When I decided to become a curator they were surprised as my father was a pilot for thirty years and later he resigned. He began running a high-end café and a book store by the beach. My mom helped around and was a freelance cookbook writer.

My parents were pretty much busy with their business and social life. Whereas, I began building the eagerness to travel, knowing more about various cultures, and historical sites.

I enjoyed reading various topics that could be misleading to suggest a connection between fundamental organizations and archeology, so interesting, yet political.

As I reached home, I kept my phone on my work desk and switched on the laptop. I began surfing around and going through more online recruitment sites.

Hours later, I checked my emails again and received a feedback for my applications. I wanted to reject all except one.

One of the most interesting job opportunities was teaching in Africa. A school needed an American Sociology Teacher. Although I hadn't ever taught at any school, I was keen to reply to their feedback. I was so ready to discuss further about the educational standards. Perhaps this was going to be my first extraordinary voyage as a teacher, I contemplate with excitement.

After skimming through the webpage, I noticed that the teaching was at a small village in Tanzania. OMG! If I got this job, this would all be a new adventure for me. The information did create a curiosity to know more about the facilities.

The new international school was named 'Haven Excel International School.' It was located a few kilometers away from a small village in Tanzania. The school was established seven years ago in the year of 2006. It had a basketball court, football field, an indoor swimming pool and many other recreational facilities. The school logo was abbreviated as 'HEIS.'

The objectives and the motto of the school were just like every educational institution. Nevertheless, the management had every motto conveyed perfectly. The school logo 'HEIS' was depicted as *H* stood for 'Honoring an affluent, victorious, education with novelty.'

*E* stood for 'Exercising education in an extraordinary level.' *I* stood for 'Involving and blending international standards,' and *S* stood for, 'Sophistication.'

The name of the school was catchy but how catchy would the location be? I wondered with concern.

This new interest seemed to signal a changing fate. It would be my first ever teaching job—only if I got it.

I clicked on the icon and read through the site. The school architecture was well built. Teachers had their own apartment with a good security system. The school's technology did not seem as advanced as other schools, but what mattered to me was a good curriculum, accommodation, food, safety and I was all good.

I was waiting for the feedback and was ready to travel to the other side of the world. It seemed crazy since Tanzania was way opposite to Hawaii. I was seeking for an adventurous change and had to overlook many other things like convenience and comfort.

I was enjoying my inquisitive gateway of unstoppable questions. I started to research and wanted to know more about Tanzania. I looked forward to travel and wished if I got a chance to see Mount Kilimanjaro. It would perhaps bring back the enthusiasm of a good career change. I started to write down some exciting things I could do in Tanzania.

Even though I knew I had to wait for the response from *Haven Excel International School,* I could not stop myself from exploring online. In the meantime, I discussed about traveling and teaching in Africa with my parents. They were pretty astonished I chose a country I had no clue about. I promised I would keep in touch with them if I got the job. I had enough with thinking what to do and how it should be done.

I cared less about anything. I felt I developed a feeling of being insensitive and did not want to be a cold stone. But what else could I have done after a bumpy ride. I am human and my senses would react.

I slowly began to walk on the steps of positivity after I read the book '*The Monk who sold his Ferrari.*' I had no Ferrari but I certainly had a luxurious expectation of love and high hopes. It was time to surrender to the Goddess of hope, if there was one, and in turn receive the strength to let go of some strings attached.

I made a collage of all my dreams and desires. I wanted to progress spiritually and materialistically. I embraced life as a blessing in its kind of form.

I could not understand was Edwin a blessing in disguise or the doorway to a new beginning. Perhaps it was all meant to be like the ancestors said.

After a night of peaceful sleep, I went to the café and chilled out. I ordered the café's specialty drink '*Dark Chocolate Cherry Soufflé*.' The drink was topped with marshmallows and cinnamon powder. I loved it. Whenever I drank it, I felt like I was being pulled to another paradise of a sensuous felicity.

After sipping it a few times, I noticed an update on my BlackBerry. I had received a feedback and the head of recruitment had placed an appointment. I was thrilled with exhilaration.

I headed to the counter, 'Look what your specialty drink brought to my life, mom. It has given me a green ticket. I received a response. I am called for an interview. Wohoo! So Mr. and Mrs. Preston, be happy for me. Mom I am so nervous now. I haven't taught before.'

"Ashley honey, you do have some experience about students from being a curator so go with the flow. Good luck for the interview," said Mrs. Preston with zeal.

'Thank you Mrs. Preston,' I teased. I could see my dad glancing at me through his square shaped glasses. He raised his thumb to express best of luck.

I paced toward him and hugged him. I had to prepare and dived into an array of questions.

Fortunately, the interviews were being held in Hawaii and after passing the two stages of interview, the rest of the paperwork would be taken care of in Africa.

That evening brought a new emotional twist making me feel nervous, yet thrilled for an interview, which was happening after two years. It almost felt like the first time. I was ready to shoot and sleep on time.

The morning sunshine brought about a hip and shining rendezvous with wisdom carved onto the clouds.

I was well prepared for the interview, and had made notes about Tanzania and the education there. I had a meeting in one of the business conference centers in Hawaii. As I entered to complete the requirements, I got to meet *Simone*, the ex– Sociology teacher whom I would be replacing if everything was successful. Simone had been a Sociology teacher in Haven Excel International School for two years for the high school level and after the contract expired she decided to come back to Hawaii.

She was offered a job position as the head of Sociology and Anthropology department in a university.

I was pleased to meet her and know more about the school. I received a positive response and began being more sure of the job. I simply hoped I was able to teach and not end up with a pack up scenario. The imagery led to an obsession of an enticing change.

After waiting for an hour I was called in. I was interviewed and asked to demonstrate some lesson plans. My enthusiasm and creativity was appraised to my surprise. I was told to wait for five days for the second stage interview and later the management would take the next step.

When I came out of the meeting room, I felt like a plate of grilled hotdogs was on my head. I was feeling restless and had a bad headache. This stage seemed to have gone well. I was eager to know what the response would be.

On the way back home, I stopped by the beach. I craved for something sweet, so parked my car and bought a strawberry cheesecake ice cream with a chocolate fudge topping. I walked along the seashore and sat down on the sand for a while.

I began talking to myself in my mind. I felt split up to various people asking several questions and could feel that there was a conference going on in there.

The questions started off as, 'Would she ever be able to forget Edwin? If yes, How? Could she be able to feel the need to have a father in a child's life? If I get the job at Haven Excel International School, would it give me an opportunity to achieve my goals? How would Tanzania actually be? The children may turn to dislike her. She had read and heard from her students about the strange eating habits. Would she also be adopting the peculiar eating habits? I wanted to scream. I needed a normal and sensible life.'

During my so called conference—the meeting in the mind was distracted with a noble thought of the betterment to follow my heart. At this moment going to Tanzania made so much sense. I could feel a positive vibe and an everlasting flow of a bold journey. I loved the challenge and it was a matter of only a two years contract.

I got up and paced towards my car. I was looking forward for the phone call. 'Five days to go baby,' I murmured.

On the way home, I went to the gym to cancel my membership, so I could change location and start fresh.

While I was signing some papers, somebody tapped my shoulder. I turned around and it was my ex-colleague, Pedro.

'I am glad to see you. We haven't met for a year. What have you been up to?' I asked with excitement.

"Likewise, oh . . . I heard about the break up. So cancelling membership?" replied Pedro with concern.

'Yes. I so need to start fresh. The new place will refresh my life. I should be going back to work soon—looking forward for that.'

"Great! I have left the museum and now working at an art gallery. It's been a few months. We should meet for coffee . . ."

While we were talking, it seemed like the devil had appeared unexpectedly. Edwin arrived and saw Pedro. I could see him pacing towards us. He seemed to just finish with his workout.

Edwin glanced at Pedro, "How are you? Been a while, dude."

"Yes, dude," replied Pedro with sarcasm.

I was feeling uncomfortable and tried to calm myself down. What's with the dude thing, I thought.

I wanted to tell Edwin, 'Why are you even talking to people I know?' I was getting annoyed and began thinking pessimistically. I did not say anything and remained mum.

I heaved a sigh and glanced towards Edwin.

"We should meet for coffee atleast at your café? So there would be no excuses," said Pedro and winked. He took out his new name card and gave it to me.

Even though I did not want to empathize myself, all those memories came back slam on my face. Trying to ignore that moment, I hugged Pedro and whispered, 'We will meet. No worries.'

He left, leaving me behind with Mr. Ego.

Edwin did not leave. He looked at me and asked, "So Ashley Preston, how have you been? It's been months."

'I am doing great. Thanks to you. I have managed to balance everything now. The old relationship seems like crap, a cheap and smelly old pair of socks. Anyway . . . how have you been? Oh, let me ask, have you kissed anyone lately?' I replied with sarcasm.

Edwin smiled and said, "Your sarcasm and frankness has always been admired and FYI I did kiss someone on the cheeks. It was Anna, my sister and it was for her birthday. Before you create this quick network in your mind that we even had sex and blah blah . . . so your birthday is coming up. What are you planning to do?"

'Oh yeah, my networking was always normal and sensible. It began to get shallow and suspicious after your *'Just a kiss'* theory began. I don't get it. Why am I even talking to you?'

"Nevermind, be normal and sensible then. Your birthday! I was going to call you for coffee. We did not work. You called it 'Chapter Closed.' Fine with me! But I don't want to be enemies.

We can dislike the whole situation and you can dislike me. But I have never felt I betrayed you. I still want to be friends . . . atleast we can be a common acquaintance. What say?" asked Edwin with honesty.

'You never betrayed me! Your kiss parade was—BETRAY! Phew! Fine, a common acquaintance—sounds like I can grant a charitable friendship of normalcy. Coffee, I shall think about it. I am kind of pleased that you have grown sensitive towards other people's feelings. I hope I am not wrong, again. I shall call you myself one day before my birthday. I am glad to celebrate the death of my thirty second birthday. It did bring this huge pay back of Karma or something. I am now trying to overlook it and see things are brighter again. We shall meet, I guess . . .' I said and continued with my paper work.

"You better do," I will be waiting. I got to go for a shower, now," said Edwin and left.

I could feel the tension easing as he did not create any drama. So, now I shall be meeting him probably for the last time. Let's see! I contemplate.

CHAPTER 3

# The death of Thirty-two

It was past noon and I was wondering why does a feedback have to take so long? I had this ominous feeling. I started to get all bugged and before I could walk down the negative lane I chose to go to the café.

Such a crazy feeling of this superstition I created of wanting to have my specialty drink 'Dark Chocolate Cherry Soufflé.'

Meeting mom at the café was nice and told her that being thirty two had its own mystery. I was definitely getting paranoid and all psychological, more than that I had a gridlock of thoughts that was making me feel uncomfortable.

After gazing at the computer disapprovingly for a couple of minutes, I simply ordered the drink. Strangely, I could also feel very creative, and wanted to try a hand at poetry or fiction. But then took a piece of paper and started drawing different types of birds. Knowing I was not a good artist and sucked at it, my determination to the attempt of completing the drawing was apprising. I realized how bad it was that even a five year old would draw better than me.

I then wanted to have a feast of various carbs together to dissolve this uneasy feeling, only if it helped. I turned around to see the view of the beach from the café. After a few seconds I received a text message. What I was waiting for had gotten my attention. I had also passed the second interview and could hear echoes derisively. Ignoring the pondering notions, I stood up and dodged on the side of the path with joy that left a smile on my face.

I could not believe it actually happened and would soon be off to Tanzania. I walked quickly at a clumsy pace and told my parents about it. They were so happy.

Now that it had happened there was a lot to be done.

I wanted to celebrate my birthday before I left to Tanzania. My life was going to take a turn to a magical realism of certain patterns yet to encounter.

It was certain to expect at some point to be treated to a monologue on social and conservation responsibilities. From where I was coming there were some compelling reasons to preserve work pieces in museums of international and national repute. Now I was to enter a new pathway I never imagined doing.

But so what, what was the worry, I wanted this—so will acknowledge it with elation. I better text Edwin like I said I would do.

Coffee seemed different today. Sitting on this funky blue couch with a mug of cappuccino did not feel as aromatic as always. Obviously, I was celebrating the death of my thirty second birthday to embrace a new year.

I came out of home with full enthusiasm and was proud of what I had to offer to the world. I was courageous in my dealings as I was to face Edwin and take the time to express myself fully in a creative manner.

I felt like I had stepped on the pedal of courage and drove my ego away. It was a mere test I was going through and surely it wasn't easy to deal with the break up.

Edwin seemed happy to see me. He could see my attempt and effort to forget the pain I went through. Deep down inside he felt guilty about this whole scenario, as I could tell with his calm and empathetic gestures. It seemed he realized it was too late to do anything. He released me from the misery and another drama if he spoke about the past. He knew it, we were not meant to be together. Friendship was the key ingredient for a balanced state of mind, he considered.

He cleared his throat and took a sip of his espresso. He had this half smile facing me.

'I got a job! I am leaving to Tanzania and guess what? I am going to be teaching high school students Sociology and Anthropology there,' I updated cheerfully.

"Well, that turned out quite exciting for you. That's new. Are you ready to travel to Africa? Ashley, you are not that fond of traveling, remember. Your feet trembled and you crawled back to your den when anyone said leave Hawaii," said Edwin with a tease.

While tapping my nails on my BlackBerry, I glanced at him with a doubt, and replied with irony, 'So someone has claimed to know me so well. People change. It is fine to take a Froggy jump. I need that change.'

"Do what makes you happy. I heard that there are a lot of strange animals and creepy crawlies there. By the way your temper and insensitive attitude can scare the ghosts away. That is only if you can find any, Ashley. You know I am just trying to say, be happy and will miss you," said Edwin and winked.

'Ghost or spirits are a myth or I would say it's a superstition. Been to a few sites, working at the museums for years and read articles, journals on people about the past. I never came across anything like that. You are the living soul and we all need to do our good willingly and unconditionally. Edwin, this is not the world of Harry Potter or Twilight or even Vampire Diaries. Sometimes, I find all this so screwed up because all this has messed up the youth's mind and I have even seen how adults go gaga about all that. About the creativity part—phenomenon—an imagination that feeds on people's mind. I like that. Spirits—not quite. But if it is all an act of paranormal activities—hmm—that can be doubtful. It gives me a second thought. You did make me think about it . . . anyway, will let you know if I ever see a ghost. If that ever happens! It is like waiting to see pigs fly.'

Giving a jovial pat, Edwin said, "You're denying the fact that there is no spirit. Wait till you see one someday. You told me once about your visit to Turkey for an archaeological coursework and watched *'The night in the museum'* five times. You felt you saw something or could see a group of people around you while you were testing samples of fossils. You found this strange amulet carving and then threw it away as it passed on an electric current. Just admit it. It was a shock and you know." His smirk indicated some truth.

'Come to think about this. I am sure this is all scientific. Let's not get there. Turkey was a coursework that was conducted seven or eight years ago. I am not a professional archeologist now. I could have been one. But I got into the limelight of still objects and there was no looking back. Today is the death of thirty two and the birth of thirty three. Can we focus on that?' denied Ashley.

"Why say death? Give yourself some credit and the merit of coming this far. Happy Birthday lady, to a person I know with charisma and magnetism not a pot full of unripe assumptions and devaluation of life. So it is not death, Ashley," praised Edwin.

'It is death. What I mean to say is goodbye to misery. There is always a rebirth to a new age and if it is not there, there shall be another death. I did learn so much during the life of thirty two. Today, we say cheers to Tanzania and goodbye to spirits and ghosts. You better not create those unwanted fear which does not exist, Edwin. Thanks for being here. Please be normal,' I replied apprehensively.

"Yes, I shall be normal and cheers to Tanzania. You must have done your research," he said with worry. His mouth curves in a reminiscent smile.

'I have. Thank you. There are so many technical aspects to read about and understand. You know Sociology-*Marxism, Weber or even Durkheim's theories* they are not my cup of tea. Let's see when I am in Tanzania. Good to see you today and thanks for being encouraging. I so needed the moral support,' I said and stood up.

I paced toward him giving him a side hug.

I did not get so lost in my ideas that temporarily lost touch with the material world. Our conversation was interesting and I was glad I didn't kill him. I leaped up and left the venue with ease.

The feeling to say goodbye to him without feeling insignificant had vanished.

I was ready to pack.

On my way home, I was thinking about all the fun and creative things I would do with the children. Everything seemed exciting.

When I reached home, I took out all my clothes from the wardrobe. I took out the diary and started jotting down all the stuff I needed for my next professional experience.

After organizing my thoughts on the papers I went on Twitter to tweet to a bunch followers who made me feel significant and were sure to read about my new job.

I Tweeted: *Tanzania, here I come.*

The expansive feeling I was undergoing was way too far from reality. I had planned to balance my whimsical nature.

Eventually that night after noting down all about my necessities and dinner with parents, I went through some important journals and articles. I separated them and put them into brown envelopes. I had four days to pack and did not want forget to take my lucky charm bracelet.

I recall that day when I completed my undergrad; I met a stranger during my coursework in Turkey. We became friends and he gave me an evil eye bracelet. I was told that in many Mediterranean cultures, people are superstitious about an evil eye. I never believed in evil eye but respected the Turkish man's belief. Since then I never separated the evil eye bracelet from me. I have taken it as my lucky charm. The bracelet was made up of red, blue and white stones. It did look so elegant to ward off negativity, but it was fascinating.

That night I got my act right by thinking towards a new dimension. My things would get stale if I kept doing the same things over and over again. I packed some stuff and went off to sleep.

The day had arrived and I was at the *Honolulu International Airport.* After saying my goodbyes and checking in my luggage, I went to buy a book. I made sure I spoke to no one and was not going to be lured into any emotional manipulative trap. I kept reminding myself, 'Focus lady, Focus.'

I had bought some magazines instead, and walked to my seat in business class. My heart was beating so fast. I had never traveled out of USA for a work experience. My trip always involved project assignments, or vacation purposes.

I sat down and quickly surveyed around the business class. I looked out the window as it was ready for takeoff. I texted my parents and switched off the phone. I decided to write down my experience from Hawaii to Tanzania and have a good sleep.

It would be a long flight to *France,* I wondered. That was a sudden decision made when I bought my tickets. My keen interest to see France first before going to Africa was getting me thrilled developing a network of illusions. And spending so quality time with me.

I sipped coffee and slowly closed my eyes. Even with a sip of coffee I could easily fall asleep. I was in my Kingdom of Tanzania. My mind had created certain places and thought it looked that way. I had no clue what my journey would be like? Who would? It was all like a puzzle.

After a few hours I woke up. I asked for a glass of white wine. I took out my diary and penned down my expectations and goals.

My first stop over was France and had planned to stay there for three days. Then my second stop over was Egypt.

Staying two days in Egypt was fine with me. Then I planned to take a direct flight to Zanzibar in Tanzania. From Zanzibar I would travel an hour by rail to '*Haven Excel International School.*' Zanzibar portrayed a unique painting on photos. I was yet to see the uniqueness in actuality.

I hadn't any well designed travel itinerary or brochures, so looked forward to see France, since I had heard so much about it. For not traveling for the longest time, I considered this as a good start to see the world.

My goals and expectations were way too long. When I went back to read it, I started to smile, and quickly looked behind my seat to see if there was anyone peeping. My personal feeling of embarrassment made me feel conscious.

There were still many hours to go until I reached France. I wanted to be rescued. The long hour flight was getting me agitated. There was a great emotional surge of intense energy. I wanted to get off the plane that very minute and see France. All I could think of was salvation. I knew it—mastery of a skill comes when one has the guts to always be taking it to the next level. The gateway to change, have an adventure and accomplishing at a great job ahead was the entire thing I was thinking about.

I was hoping that Tanzania would be my sanctuary where I could feel at home and be myself. I sipped my wine, and was ready to connect with new people around me. At that point of time, freedom and salvation were dancing in my mind.

The sole interest to embrace a new lifestyle did bring a fleeting thought of concern where I began judging my decision of taking up an opportunity I doubted now. I marveled with the facts and notions that simply took me for granted and I tried to chuck it out of my mind.

The worm of expectation was killing me.

# CHAPTER 4

# Salvation

Salvation was not exactly what I needed. However, my flashback to my relationship with Edwin needed salvation. It was a great feeling to be with someone whom one would think as the marriage material. But who knows that it could be a temporary indication, until there is a flashlight of true colors in relation to behavioral mannerisms. Perhaps something better was stored with a cherry on top.

It was not so easy to forget, especially when one is still very much up in the air. By then I drank three glasses of white wine, had written about my feelings and drawn out of shape birds again. Why do I always end up drawing birds and not any other animals? This was odd and mind blowing at the same time.

The wine had already made me a little tipsy and emotional. I took out my evil eye bracelet and looked at it for a few seconds, then put it back in the bag. I wished the journey would be like a treasure hunt. The hunt would make this new experience worthwhile.

Hours passed and had managed to get some precious sleep. I had the meal that was served, and after took out the brochures that had been given to me by the flight attendant on the tourist attractions in France. I was keen to see the most common, yet extravagant Eiffel Tower in Paris. Then I planned to take a tour to give me a brief picture about this wonderful place on Earth. I knew I would be more like a backpacker; however, three days would give me a good perspective and a wine—dine experience the French style. I was ready to have a date with—*Moi.*

Let me put it this way; everything would surely turn out to be—*fan-fucking-tastic.*

I put away my brochures and was ready to land after I heard the announcement.

The landing was smooth and as I got out I saw someone from the hotel that came to receive me at the airport holding a board with my name on it.

The French man was young and he pronounced my name in a strange way. I felt my name sounded more like a dessert that I could savor. I greeted him and he escorted me to the taxi.

On my way to the hotel, I passed through many cathedrals and castles. Before reaching the three star hotel in Paris, I requested the chauffeur that if I could see the nearest vineyard of Champagne in Epernay. I had never seen a vineyard before, and did not want to waste any time. I offered him a good tip for his extra service. On my way, I took too many pictures.

The vineyard was quite far away from the hotel. The hours of drive got my buttocks soared, but after all the enthusiasm to see the vineyard outweighed the sensation of my soared buttocks.

I started to feel blurry and dosed off in the taxi. When we arrived, the chauffeur called my name, "*Aush-lee* instead of Ashley." I woke up and wanted to teach him some English. I ignored the pronunciation and got off the private taxi.

I ambled toward the 25,000-30,000 hectares of champagne vines. I took a video and thought of sharing it with my new class. I met a guide there and he showed me around. I noticed and wrote about different types of grapes that were used for champagne. The chauffeur also accompanied me as he found the whole scenario interesting and artistic.

I began tasting different types of champagne. The champagne tasted so good that I could not let go off it. I could also feel that I would end up sleeping on the vineyard. All I needed was a bed.

I offered an extra glass to the chauffeur and told him, 'You must be used to this.'

He smiled and said, "Yes madam in French, *Oui, madame.*"

I giggled and added, 'Your language is like a song—Nice.' I did not want to spend too much time at the vines. Two hours had passed there, and then the long drive back would make my ass look like a watermelon eventually because of nourishing it to becoming fat, I thought.

I left to the hotel and was waiting for nice hot shower.

I ticked champagne vines out from my list in the taxi. Now I wanted to see a cathedral and a castle. I could not believe where my energy was coming from. Noticing the view from the taxi, I began having loads of ideas. I could toy with the idea of visiting faraway places, maybe in a company of a lover. I hoped for a change and salvation from old memories. I realized that the true understanding of the situation comes only from the heart. It was better to sink into the mood of the environment around me rather than breaking it down into small sections and analyzing it. With that I was going to drown towards a new stress and not enjoy my mini-holiday.

Hours had passed and I was back in town. I was going to stay at '*Jardins Eiffel.*' It was located few moments away from the river and the Eiffel Tower. As I was nearing it, the view of the Eiffel tower in the evening was amazing. Oh damn, it looks like a sexy lady with all the shimmer.

I knew it was just a tower. When looking at it again I could not help but say, 'You are not a tower. You are art. You are history for generations with an angelic beauty. You are the fashion that stroked in the 70s and blew everyone's mind. People could fall in love or even come here for a detox.' I heaved a sigh. The chauffeur was looking at me from the mirror in front. He thought I was going crazy talking to myself.

"We are here. You can check in. I bring your luggage," said the chauffer with a smile. I went inside and did my formalities. I walked a few steps ahead then came back. I had asked the chauffer if he could take me around the city. He was very happy to do it for extra bucks. All this simply became pay and smile.

I kept my luggage on the bed and could see the view of the Eiffel Tower. It could be compared to a good dessert. One could not stop looking at it. It looked huge but I couldn't make out how big it would be. I turned around, took out my camera, and began clicking away. The tower was and will always be a beauty.

I was done taking pictures. Now it was time to scan the room for its cozy beauty.

Even if the room was not too big, it was well decorated and homely. The room had everything I needed. The art work around the room was like I was sipping coffee at the art gallery. It was so mesmerizing.

'Wow! I am here,' I said loudly and jumped on the bed.

I knew I could not waste more time so changed and had put on my peach colored satin dress. I took the camera and some champagne chocolates I had bought earlier.

I walked down the stairs and was seeing the interiors of the hotel. I began finding the chauffer. I waited for a few minutes and he had walked into the hotel. We then left and were touring around the city. It was so nice to see many chilled out places and bars. The pleasure of taking pictures was like a virus.

Driving around for a while got me tempted to have wine again. I bought a bottle of *Rosé* and was drinking it in the taxi assuring the chauffer that I would be careful.

We reached the Eiffel tower. It felt like heaven. The picture taking session was uncontrollable that I could feel my tears come down my eyes.

I began to feel that I did not know what I was getting into. Was teaching in Africa my solution? It is not going to be so beautiful like Paris. What about dating? I need to see yummy people around once in a while or even be the delicacy in his life.

I sat by at a nearby café for a while and was simply glaring at the mesmerizing piece of art. Hmm . . . so would I be this desiring and delicious dessert in any man's life. Would I be able to walk that lane again? Would the sex appeal still be in me? Oh this was all getting me pout with doubt.

I took my bag and I left the tower heading back to the hotel.

Getting back to the hotel felt like I had left something so precious behind and imprinted memorable memories in return.

Having had a long day I ordered from room service. I ate and stepped into the tub I had set ready for a bubble bath. I closed my eyes and reminded to be true to myself at all times or else I would find myself in situations that would lead to discomfort and frustration. A feeling of relief brought a smile that I started humming something out of tune. I took a deep breath and said, 'I will survive.' The fluctuation of notions had surely danced its way today.

There was a strong transforming force that was directly against me. I had to find my inner sense of leadership and confidence to stand up again. If I did not be assertive sometimes and speak my mind; it would be my loss. I was so sick of this one way communication where I had to be able to be the understanding one and yes, at the end become the black sheep because of someone else's created dump. I got off the bathtub and changed.

I sprayed the vanilla room freshener and went to sleep. With my positive attitude, the two days spent in France was splendid. I saw the palace, churches and cathedrals, visited a museum, dined at a fine restaurant, sipped various coffees, shopped and finally went on my so called date on the last day.

I thanked the chauffeur for a wonderful insight of the city and took him out for dinner. The so called date with the chauffeur was not appealing whatsoever. It was more like filling in the space of a companion over a relishing dinner and a partner to clink the glass of wine with. We laughed and shared many stories. I told him I would remember him and send him a postcard when I reached Africa. The night was a tribute to a fun journey and a new beginning to my next destination, 'Egypt.'

Goodbyes' were not my thing. I did not like it as much. I noticed after I told him, the chauffeur started to smoke and was getting agitated. I took a few steps ahead. Then realized I never gave him a tip. I took a few steps backwards and the chauffeur stubbed the cigarette.

When he saw some dollars in my hand, he showed some consideration. I did what I thought was good after a great service. At the same time I knew that money played an important role when one needed to express empathy and kindness. There are no free lunches anywhere. Only if one was a refugee. Working hard to pamper one is never a want but has become a need for many.

I decided to repack everything and the clothes were spread everywhere on the bed. I kept what was important on top of the pile for the next trip. I was rushing as I had to leave for the airport. This time I decided for another chauffeur. I had enough of the first one. The feeling of boredom and freedom for a change was rising.

Hearing the phone ring; I quickly put everything back in order and left the room. I did not want to make the chauffeur wait. For a change I could feel the moment of peace in my soul. Looking at the churches, infrastructure and people made my jaw drop. The three day stay in France was fabulous and surely a fantastic stamp of happiness I would never forget.

I could feel this refreshing feeling and appreciated everything around me. I reached the airport on time. Checking in was no hassle. When there was an announcement, I got up and was eager to get to my seat. I whispered, 'Egypt, here I come.'

After keeping the laptop on the upper compartment, I asked for a glass of Rosé. After all, sitting in the business class did make me feel part of a grandiose journey. I closed my eyes for a few moments. My mind began to wonder and I could see myself watching the pyramids. I opened my eyes and sipped the wine. I had no appetite and wanted to sleep.

Time passed by so quickly. It felt like someone had just rotated the globe. Egypt was ready to welcome me. I was waiting to get my luggage and could feel something strange. I did not know what it was. I got the luggage and walked gingerly.

I got into the taxi and was ready to tour around Cairo. I had told the chauffeur to head to the hotel first. This time I chose some hotel not too far from the airport. It was a two star local motel. The service seemed good when I arrived. My room was clean and not as luxurious as the one in France. The room had cream colored walls with only one painting on it. The bed was comfortable, the shower and network was acceptable.

Stretching away, suddenly I heard this squeaky sound. The sound kept echoing from different directions. I was beginning to regret my choice of stay. I wanted to atleast have a peaceful sleep. So I walked out of my room wearing my robe. There was no such sound anywhere. It was quite strange that I could only hear it in my room.

When I went for a shower, I saw something on the wall. It seemed like someone had written a message on the wall. It was: *Stay alert! You shall receive an important message today via fax, e-mail or telephone from someone far away. A visitor is arriving from out of town.*

The message on the wall freaked me out. I looked around the bathroom. There was no one. Then I thought, maybe the message had been there for the longest time and no one ever noticed it. I splashed some water on my face and continued with my shower.

That afternoon, I went to have some *kebabs and shisha*. The kebabs tasted interesting. I interviewed the chef and the waiter. I started taking notes and sipped my virgin cocktail. The café was a few blocks away from the hotel. Surprisingly the décor was chic, with a low table surrounded by luxurious chairs and draped by colorful materials. The café was spacious and attractive.

Pages were flicked and finally the pen was put away. Pictures were taken and every flavor of the shisha was blissful. I thought of going for a walk. I walked and learnt a different lifestyle. Even though there was Pizza Hut or even McDonalds,' the people were very different. I could feel the culture shock. Strange men were staring at me. They were not yummy and I was never imagining myself to be their delicacy. I was even offered by an Arab for a ride to a bar nearby. Ignoring them was the best option.

Egyptian women were beautiful and glowing. Their flawless skin and light eyes were compelling. I had already walked two kilometers and contemplated of seeing the Sphinx and The Pyramids of Giza. So I walked back to the motel. I booked for a private tour. The chauffeur was ready to leave but I was busy taking pictures of hookahs. He requested me, "We better be there before it is night."

I walked quickly and stumbled. Then I crouched to pick up the brochures that had spread on the floor. To my surprise I noticed a vague shadow of children on the floor. When I looked up, there was no one. I knew I was not retarded. I picked up the brochures and walked towards the private taxi.

First, I see a weird message on the wall. Then I see shadows of children. Are these clues or just ways of getting me paranoid? I wondered anxiously.

On the way, I saw mudbrick homes, flat roofs and how some villagers were using the birds as food and their droppings to fertilize crops. The scene was not so attractive to me; however, every culture had its unique persona. The ride was not too long and I could see the pyramids from a distance. When the chauffeur parked the taxi, he escorted me to the entrance of the place. I had to agree that the food and places in Egypt were simply graceful and astounding.

The pyramids were huge, and I looked like a dwarf in front of them. I asked around and got a private guide to lead the way. The guide updated me about the ancient civilization. I did know deeply about the civilization, but having to see the creation was fantastic. My new job has fascinated me because I would be able to teach a little about history and know more about all sorts of people.

The picture session had started. I paid an entrance, which was so expensive, but I could not miss the opportunity.

I was briefed about the three pyramids: *Cheops, Khafre and Menakaure. Each pyramid is a different tomb to a king*. I was allowed to go to one of them after I had paid the entrance.

Before I entered the pyramid I turned around, and saw the Cairo skyline in the background. It was spectacular. Then I went inside the pyramid. I walked down the passageway and entered the room that led to the Queen's chamber. The room was finished with polished granite. As I walked further and entered the King's Chamber, I noticed every detail and the scientific approach to the building of the pyramid.

I could not take notes because there was not enough space. So took pictures instead and thought of taking notes later when I was going to Tanzania. While walking up the stairs, I saw the shadow of the children again. This time it seemed like I was being followed. With excitement, I turned around. I saw no one.

I began to feel it was a monstrous act. When I walked ahead, I saw them again. I walked faster, and they followed faster. I said it out loud, 'What on Earth are you? If you want to play, go to a park. Stop annoying me in the pyramid.'

The moment of an unsolved problem was bugging me. I could not comprehend the incidents happening to me in Egypt.

Letting out a sigh, I paced ahead and did not care about the shadows. It was nearing darkness and I had to hurry up. Carefully noticing every detail I walked out of the pyramid. The amount of walking in the pyramid made me feel like I had a good exercise.

The chauffeur was waiting outside and took me for a short drive towards the Sphinx. The Sphinx had the body of a lion and the head of a king. I was curious why was it built? Nevertheless, no one ever found out the mystery about it.

Camels were on the desert. After some point I saw tents. I entered one of the tents. Old men where selling souvenirs. The souvenirs were appealing and I ended up buying a small hookah with a feather shaped pen. No combination whatsoever, but the pen was artistic. A German couple came up to me and asked details about the pyramids. While we were talking, they mentioned that they were going to Africa after that. They were going to Zimbabwe.

I did mention about my work in Tanzania and how I was looking forward for a new challenge for freedom. I was in a hurry, so excused myself.

Why am I talking about salvation to people I do not know? Strangers are the best people to share—they don't judge—they listen—in most cases.

The moment of touring was over and I was so glad I was back at the hotel. I needed a massage badly. I went for a hot shower, sprayed the vanilla room air-freshener and went to sleep.

This time the shadow of the children gave me space from an illusion, I believe.

The morning sun's rays were shining on my legs as I could see after twisting and turning. I got up and switched on the television. I lazed around and ordered coffee and cereals. Coffee was great. I texted my parents about my interesting trip. While texting, I walked to switch on the shower faucet. Subsequently, I went back and got my scrub out from the bag.

When I walked in, the shower was switched off. I was dazed and it looked as if there was an automatic detector. I found nothing. Then looked around and saw the wall was clear. The message I had seen yesterday was vanished. Bizarre and unexpected events were occurring. I thought that the management must have painted it over and I continued with the shower.

The echoing sounds appeared simultaneously. I walked out and saw there was nothing. I dressed and began packing my stuff. I wanted to leave Egypt soon. I did not know what was going on.

On one hand, I saw beauty and on the other, I hear noises, see a strange message, and shadows of children following.

Maybe it was not my day or I had a gift. Could I actually see spirits? Oh no! I am doing too much thinking. I should stop.

As I was walking down the stairs, I geared up my positivity and was thinking of heeding the small innuendoes and possibly there was a larger picture to life. I decided to latch on this positivity before I went insane.

I paid and confirmed my check-out timing. I had the day to myself. So I went to see a museum and went for another flavored shisha.

Sitting back in the same café and writing down what I saw during my short trip was remarkable. I managed to spend some quality time with myself. Who knows that was what I really needed. I did not need to please anyone but myself.

The time to check-out was near and my mind was wondering again. I was experiencing a bit of restlessness and saw the shadow of children again before I entered the motel. I was unsure of what I was supposed to do.

My mind was sharp and logical. With these incidents it was difficult for me to think straight. I stride straight into the room, get my stuff and leave for Tanzania.

All I could think was—Shadows!

Were these children, angels? Or are they dead? Maybe it is an illusion. Time was to tell who they really were, I presumed.

The crazy network of analyzing or jumping into conclusions a mind does, simply made my normalcy go kaput.

# CHAPTER 5

# Electrifying

I placed my hand luggage in the overhead compartment and sat on the aisle seat of the economy class. When I closed my eyes for a few seconds, I heard voices rising to the most penetrating shriek in my ear. I opened my eyes, and felt a sort of small electrical shock that woke me up terrified and my heart beating quickly.

The seat belt sign was on that I couldn't stand up, but gradually turned my head sideways to see if there were any children around. To my surprise, there were no children, but a group of middle age men were staring at me. I looked away and started to take a deep breath.

My decision to take the job began to prickle my confidence that I had to see the bright side. My pondering thoughts began to make me realize that I was wavering so much about a decision that even after I had made it, I was hesitant about following through with it. How strange can this get, I knew it would be difficult for me to find the assurance that I was looking for, till then inevitably I fell down the slippery slope of self-doubt.

What the F . . . is wrong with me? Is my decision to have children beginning to haunt me? I wonder with dismay.

I remembered my conversation with Edwin on ghosts and tried hard to deny the fact that maybe I was on the verge to have a slight belief in it.

By then the plane had taken off and I was having roasted peanuts with a glass of apple juice. My keen interest and enthusiasm toward the excitement of a new job was juggling in my mind. I found that there was an abstemious, conservative tone to the day that was stealing the fuel from the fire to a massive change.

I freed my hair from its elastic band, quickly combing it out through my fingers, and then twisted it back into place.

While sipping apple juice, I took out my camera and went through the pictures taken in France and Egypt. The moments of an artistically developed city were captured in celluloid. I couldn't believe my photographic skills. I certainly did improve big time. I then put away the camera and gave my empty glass to the flight attendant.

Hearing to the announcement on landing at Zanzibar International Airport, I put my seat back to an upright position, and closed my eyes for a few seconds. The few moments of silence sent a pleasant sensation of peace. My usual exuberant nature was far more subdued than my normal personality. I was wishing to spend the entire evening watching whatever came on TV.

Knowing I was spending the night in Zanzibar and had half a day on the following day, I considered touring around and knowing something about the culture. When I landed, I quickly wore my evil eye bracelet and paced quietly toward the exit of the plane. Internally I felt like I was maintaining my inner peace without squelching the fire.

After getting my luggage, I walked toward the chauffer who was holding a board with my name on it. I didn't say much and sat in the private taxi.

To my astonishment, the island was pretty with beaches around and the people were helpful when I checked into the hotel in Stone Town. The affordable priced Pearl Palace Hotel had an incredible architecture mostly with cream and peach colored theme design.

As I entered the room, I noticed the wooden furniture and placed my hand bag on the dressing table. I tipped the bellboy and simply sat on the bed. Slowly stretching my hand, yawning, I was lying on the cream colored pillow. I could see the flashing fluorescent lights from my bedroom, and began to feel drowsy.

Without realizing what time it was, I went off to sleep for a few hours. Hearing a hollow squeaking sound of a door woke me up. I opened my eyes, took another pillow and hugged it. I recalled moments when I saw the shadows of the children. I got up and began to survey the room. Noticing it was not a big room and from a distance a Mosque could be seen. I went over to the dressing table and went through some brochures on must see attractions.

Having put a check market on the *Anglican Cathedral, Slave Market, House of Wonders,* and some restaurants, I went to take a shower.

Feeling fresh, I decided to go to the cafe.

I took my key card, wallet, and paced out the door heading toward the staircase. I walked down the stairs, since I was on the second floor. As I entered the coffee shop named, *Bonga Bonga,* I sat next to the window pane where I could see the street and people stroll outside.

There was a pungent fragrance of spices like cloves and cinnamon. Surveying the menu, I ordered the traditional *Chips-my-eye.* I was told it is a chip omelet, where Chips are placed into a shallow frying pan and as they sizzle away two beaten eggs are poured over the top. This is then cooked into a solid omelet, stuffed with chips and various spices. It sounded too yummy that I had to try one.

In the mean time, there was a troupe of dancers ready to sway to *Taarab.*

Taarab was a type of music originated in Zanzibar, and natives believed that people got closer to their ancestors when they performed it.

I was curious since I knew little about it. My limited knowledge about Zanzibar was the experience of rapid social changes of a large number of immigrants and the end of slavery. As the century progressed, there was a desire to be seen as Swahili in the 1910's, and there was a switch to ethnic identification. Years passed by, and the progress towards modernization brought about a big social change in Zanzibar.

One should come to Zanzibar to taste the phenomenal change of modernization which is amazing for tourists, I noticed.

It became a calmer disposition like the afternoon which made it easier for a person to handle favors and requests with his or her customary grace. I saw cuisine be placed on the table, and I ordered iced milk coffee to balance the taste of spices.

The *Chips-my-eye* was quite tasty and exceeded my expectation. I could chew it and regurgitate it and eat it again. The crinkled eyes, creased brow, and the aroma of bitter sweet coffee with vanilla flavored whip cream brought a self-satisfied grin on my face. I simply love food. This was not a pass at one go. I wanted to eat it again someday.

The sound of a loud thump on the drums got my attention. I looked at a group of male dancers dancing at midnight on a fusion of Arabic and Indian-style vocals. The DJ played hardcore gangsta rap music that was well synchronized with the dance.

The dance went on for a couple of minutes, and I was in a jovial mood to try the traditional Tanzanian beer suiting the reggae music moment later. Having a few sips of the beer gave me a headache and I was not feeling too good. I ordered the delicate banana custard chilled that was served in a wine glass for dessert.

When I ate it, I finally felt my senses back, and went back to my room. I was in no stamina to change my clothes and slept.

At around four in the morning, the multiple-pane windows appeared to be misty leaving a self constructed smile on the window. The shadows disappeared and the smile had condensate to blood droplets, like a tear drop.

The ambience being misty got me feeling quite hot during dawn. After twisting and turning, I managed to get some sleep and woke up for breakfast.

I called room service for salmon croquettes with a traditional spinach salad served with mash potatoes, and a cup of cappuccino.

Removing my clothes from the bag, and tying my hair into a bun, I noticed a red colored blotch on the window. Thinking of what it was, I concluded it might be paint and simply went to spray Vitamin E Face Mist on my face. The slight fragrance of rose water brought about instant refreshment.

The knock on the door got my taste buds watery indicating my desire to a great appetite. The waiter placed the meal on the table and left. I sprinkled brown sugar in my cappuccino and sipped it. I felt really relaxed and began writing my agenda for the day.

I called the receptionist for a private taxi to visit the Anglican Cathedral, Slave Market, and the House of Wonders. I then continued with eating my breakfast. The salmon croquettes and traditional spinach salad were different. The regular type of spinach was not used, I presumed and the croquettes had a crunchy, spicy, and fulfilling taste.

I looked toward the window again, and wondered what the red colored blotch really was. Being controlled by various thoughts, I stood up and walked toward the window as if I was hypnotized by a magnetized pull. I let out a sigh and noticed an inexplicable absurdity. The word *Kar . . .* was being traced on the misty window. I was so perplexed with the nonchalant threat I assumed to be.

My heart beating faster and feeling too cold in the room was unusual. No one was around even outside the window. An incomplete word was being delineated that evoked an unpleasant feeling. There was a tight pressing feeling behind my cheekbones, and my bottom lip was trembling.

Suddenly the phone rang in the room and I turned around. After a couple of rings, I paced toward the phone and picked it up. It was a call from the receptionist about the private taxi being arrived.

I rubbed my right eye and saw the window. It wasn't misty at all, which seemed like it evaporated within a few seconds. I went for a quick shower and packed all my belongings.

The excellent breakfast didn't do justice after all a frightful incident. Something just had to happen to trigger my patience.

I sprayed the classic Chanel perfume and slid it back in my hand bag. While I was taking my stuff, I surveyed the room and was deeply wondering about the incident.

I kept my head high and muttered, 'Whatever it was! I am not scared. You need help, so find someone else. But maybe ghosts might exist or was it a spirit of someone who died in this room . . . Oh, no!'

I took my stuff without even any help of the bellboy and headed to the elevator. I entered the elevator managing to take my luggage inside and pressed no. 1.

As I came out, I began dragging the luggage, and the bellboy came to assist me.

Placing my Gucci handbag on the receptionist's desk, I gave him the keycard and asked a few questions regarding the Anglican Cathedral, Slave Market, and the House of Wonders.

I left my luggage in the concierge and sat in the taxi. I spoke to the chauffeur with a goatee and was taken to see the Anglican Cathedral.

On my way I saw some old built universities and some local restaurants. I felt sleep deprived. Now the importance of sleep was simply the first priority.

I reached the cathedral and as usual captured lovely pictures. I got out off the taxi and continued walking towards the combination of Gothic and Arabic styles known for its Basilica shape and barrel crypt roof. The cathedral was quite old and depicted a symbol of slavery.

I overheard a guide about the site being originally a slave market. The cathedral was near a tree where slaves were tied and beaten. Having heard that, I quickly surveyed around and paced toward the other end to take some pictures. While clicking, I felt like someone's arms were around my waist giving me a warm hug. The feeling was strange and akin to steam like sensation in my blood. The hug began to get tighter and as if I was having a strong force to turn around.

I looked downwards and saw nothing. Slowly, I looked at the tree from a distance for a few seconds. The tree seemed like any common tree. I closed the camera lens and put it inside the hand bag. There was something about the cathedral. The deep pain of the past and the victory of overcoming slavery reflected as I saw the sun's rays shining on the window pane.

I began to squint and this untapped resource of the past got me to think about the lives of the people who merely became the puppet of powerful people. I glanced at my watch and considered going to the Slave Market.

Sitting in the taxi, I noticed a squirrel on my seat. I squealed and saw it jump out of the window then running up the tree.

Having the desire to scream loudly and wondering what the heck just happened, I blurted, 'Keep the windows closed at all times.' The driver apologized and started the engine.

Within a few minutes I had arrived to the market which was located nearby.

When I got off, I was quite stunned with the place.

One of the guides was holding a big wooden board that had a brief history about the slaves. I began reading what was carved on the board:

***Late 1800's Dr. Livingston made a request to eliminate slavery and the brutal trafficking of humans by means of the Stone town market.***
***People from Tanzania, Malawi, Zambia and innumerable other nations where sold at auction to Arabs.***
***There were two slave chambers, a larger one for women and children and a smaller one for the men.***
***All slaves would have to spend three days in cramped and atrocious conditions to divide the weak from the strong . . .***

I couldn't read any longer and pictured the whole scenario. I walked toward the chamber and could see it being dark. I could feel the tears of every person suffering and pleading to be liberated.

I was so glad I was living in the world of modernization and slavery was just read in books. We became the slaves of our heart and desires at times.

I hoped slavery never came back.

Fidgeting with my lucky charm bracelet, I left the chambers. The thrill to see Zanzibar had become true and the history only read in books was finally seen. There were no regrets and I was ready to visit the House of Wonders. My emotions were churning in my stomach.

When I visited the museum, it certainly depicted leadership, art, history, that revealed a rich story of the past well portrayed for tourists and locals.

I couldn't believe that it was time to leave Zanzibar and get to the village I could pass through to reach the school. I was trying to recall the name of the village but couldn't.

I took my luggage and sat on the ferry. I was finding the paper with the name of the village, which I had to show the agent whom I was meeting on the other end of the island.

The wild beast migration from one place to another is nature's greatest act where an individual got to muster up all the confidence and take the risk to move on and all the desperate and bloody drama has to come to end for the next scene to start.

Until then, my innocence and ignorance to the other side of the island depicted a person waiting patiently to meet nature's next act.

CHAPTER 6

# Getting to—HAVEN

Although calm is welcome, detachment is not justified. Everything seemed too good to be true. I packed my bags and simply traveled miles away thinking I would escape problems. There were promising signs of reform all over my head, but moving from an acute to an unceasing phase was way beyond my judgment.

Sitting on the ferry filled with too many people got me edgy. It was like a bucket filled with many frogs trying to leap for a spacious movement. I pressed my fingers on my knees and took a deep breath. The strange smell from outside created an unpleasant aroma of salty perspiration.

I took out the paper from my handbag to check the name of the village. I read the village name, *Bondeni* and recited the name incase I got lost.

After hearing the horn of the ferry, I knew it was time to reach. I stood up next to my luggage. I looked around and saw that I was nowhere near luxury.

I stepped down the ferry and dragged my luggage. I noticed a Black man of about five foot ten inches holding a paper with my name. I went forward and he told me he was here to receive me. His enunciation was not very clear and spoke English quite less. I managed to understand him and asked him about the school.

His eyes flashing in anticipation, his lips quivered, and he replied, "My name is Charlie. Welcome to Africa. I will be your agent and guide for today. Going to the school will take more than one hour. We have to travel towards the end of this village by rail and after a twenty minute ride, you will reach the school."

'Oh, I didn't know the school was quite far from the city?' I said with apprehension.

"The school is big and hopefully, you don't miss the city," said Charlie politely.

Charlie took my luggage and we sat in the car to the train station.

On my way, we saw people live in floorless shacks made of corrugated metal or unstable planks just barely held together.

I smiled at Charlie and was out of words. I was in no position to express anything. My life had certainly changed and the globe had rotated to a destination where I was building an airy castle of confidence.

Holding a Gucci bag resembled nothing but a world of materialistic pleasures where some could not even afford a plate of a decent chicken curry with rice. If I was to compare life, I know I was better off than many people.

We reached the railway station and were walking towards the compartment. Now a single shrill trumpet echoed from afar in the midst of the trombones and the dull spin of the drums were increasing every moment. I turned around and noticed that there was no one playing any sort of instruments.

The sounds of the blend of instruments felt like someone was being welcomed with grace.

Why is it always my ears? Goodness! I think curiously.

I entered the train and sat down on my seat. I began to get anxious as the train was nearing the destination. I grinned at Charlie and looked out the window. Then I looked at the empty seat next to me. The train obviously looked old and was traveling at a very slow pace.

Charlie grounded his knuckles into his cheek, squishing one side of his face, and leaned towards the window pane. I place my hands flat on the table and slightly smiled. I could see the conductor coming to ask for the ticket.

Charlie handed him the ticket and asked me, "Would you like to have coffee? You can try the traditional black coffee of Africa."

'Sure, I would like to,' I replied politely.

Charlie got up and went towards the pantry where beverages where being prepared for passengers. He bought two cups of coffee and walked back to the seat.

I took the coffee in the cream colored plastic cup and sipped the coffee. The taste was perfect and not too strong.

'Thank you. This is good,' I complimented.

I added, 'How long have you been working as an agent for the school?'

"It has been a few years. I am beginning to like it and I don't think I will change my job now," replied Charlie.

'Great, so what did you work as before?' I asked with concern.

"Hmm . . . I own a small supermarket. But now I hired someone to look after it, and my wife also takes care of it. I applied for this job for extra income. I am planning to shift to another city in Africa with better facilities," described Charlie.

'Wish you well and I think we have reached,' I said jovially. I could feel my lip corners stretched sideways.

"Yes, we have. Please walk towards the left and watch your step," said Charlie with care.

I stepped down the train and took a deep breath. I noticed that there were not many people around. I walked dragging my hand luggage, as Charlie was carrying my big suitcase.

There was a lanky old man, with arms like twigs. His feet resembled shovels. He had buck teeth that stuck out and smiled contently at me like a grinning bunny. He said, "Welcome, Mam. I am your driver, Cooky. Let me help you with the luggage."

I handed him the luggage and sat in the private taxi. I glanced at Cooky and was noticing his buck teeth. He surely looked like a rabbit. What kind of name was Cooky, I thought.

The awkward smell in the taxi made me feel giddy. I couldn't distinguish the strong odor.

Charlie was sitting in the front with the driver. His head moved left then right several times before he blurted, "We will reach in twenty minutes. HAVEN is located near this remote village called *Burgamal*. You will not find many people here. But HAVEN is one of the best schools here."

'What does Burgamal mean?' I asked.

"Burga means from the town. Mal has no particular meaning. I can't recall the history behind this name, but precisely, Burgamal attracts many tourists and people from the town or city. With the international school being located here, it has improved the education standard for our people."

'I see. Indeed, it is quite unique and it makes it even more exciting to see this place,' I stated with enthusiasm.

There was silence until I reached the Burgamal. The village was certainly not quite big. One could presume that the population would not be more than five hundred people. There was a clinic, a few local marts and children played on the streets.

The difference of place and of course the change in ambience got me to think of various things. I tittered, covering my mouth with a slim hand when I saw children playing with mud and a basketball. They needed a better thing to play with. But it was so cute how they were so indulged with their game.

The driver drove up the hill and black smoke flowed out the rotten tail pipes like the smoke out of an old pipe.

"We are here. We'll get your luggage," informed Charlie.

The mountainous ranges and cool weather in the evening was soothing. Stepping down from the vehicle I could see a cave like entrance.

Charlie was holding my luggage and I followed him toward the cave.

In front of me were a few trees. It was like a lone secluded island. It looked as if it were a boat, attempting to escape to tranquil waters.

I continued walking into the cave. It was lit with lamps and simply looked like one was entering a Harry Potter studio.

The interior inside was a mixture of various brick colors like cream, white, peach, red, brown, and yellow. The combination was interesting and not common. As I passed though the cave, I saw the big board where the initials HAVEN were imprinted. It did stand out and looked marvelous. It denoted the significance of education and the collaboration of youthful souls fostering a better future.

To my right, I saw the serviced apartment of approximately ten floors which was for the teachers. I was awed by the facility and was wondering how it would be inside.

As I paced ahead, noticed that I was walking downwards a slope. About a hundred meters I saw this huge mansion like school.

It was a blend of a peachy, brown, and cream colored architecture from outside. The school from the exterior did look welcoming and was hard to believe a school like that was built near a remote village.

It seemed like a small city within a city.

"Zuri, bugs and rodents love books. The worst offenders include cockroaches, mice and termites. The library will naturally have fewer critters if it is kept clean. So cover them and be careful," said Elma.

Letting out a sigh, "Just look at him, you are crowing about all the books," Elma mumbled.

I stopped and overheard their conversation. To my notice the janitor was frowning and holding a feather duster in his hand.

The young woman turned around and saw me. Everything seemed flopped and she was pretty upset when she saw me prying their conversation.

Her tresses of silky blonde hair were fit neatly into a stunning chignon. Her deep-set chocolate brown eyes looked at me. Dimples were pressed under her high cheekbones as she introduced herself.

"My name is *Elma Sadik*. I was told about you. You must be Ashley Preston. I hope you had a great journey coming here. I am the Science teacher here for the upper primary and secondary level. I shall escort you to the principal's office."

'Sorry didn't mean to pry. I just heard someone talking loudly so it got my attention. Nice to meet you,' I said respectfully.

I smiled at her and I freeze as I entered the corridors of the school. To my left was the library where I could see from its huge doors that different kinds of students from different ethnicities were sitting with their friends studying. The massive windows at the back of the library gave a stupendous look. It was well architected. The artificial trees and plants standing in almost every corner with angelic monuments around the library was unique.

What the hell was this? It was like the European architecture was well infused and blended in Africa.

It was overwhelming and so good to be true.

I was keen to enter the library, but continued walking with Elma towards the principal's office.

"You can go inside. She is waiting for you," said Elma and left.

I opened the door and could hear the fire crackling, the principal was hushing some students at her room to behave, occasionally someone turning the page, and some chair abrading against the floor.

I was stunned because it looked like another high-tech library with ancient British interior. I recalled the moment where I had watched Harry Potter and The Chronicles of Narnia, with all the amazing art and magic. As for this one, it was pure reality with a touch of magic where some things were technology driven that seemed magical.

The students left the room and *Principal Orchestra Ruiz* welcomed me cordially. I was offered a cup of hot coffee and briefed about my responsibilities and the role every teacher played at HAVEN.

I glimpsed at the red haired woman whose hair was tied in a ponytail and had hazel eyes. I then surveyed around the room quickly and loved the interior. She seemed in her early forties and looked pretty. 'Your office is so cool. It is well decorated and it's nice,' I said with hesitation.

"Yes . . . indeed. I have been working here ever since this school started and this school is a caliber of its own manifestation. These are our materials about the history of the school, policies, curriculum and facilities provided for the teachers. You may take a tour around the school and rest at your room. Remember not to pry at or on something or someone that is not your business."

'Umm . . . Sure, I would mind my own business. Thank you Mrs. Orchestra and I shall make a move. I will take my schedule from the staff's office and see it from there,' I said and turned around to leave the room.

I should have just been an interior decorator. What a beauty and I love the designs. I wonder how the church would be. I contemplated.

I opened the door and stepped out. As I walk, I passed a few tables where students were sitting and chatting. To my left, I notice on the table sat a beautiful red colored bowl and unsophisticated in design.

As I looked inside, I saw on the bottom of the bowl a hot, tender brownie loaded with macadamia nuts. On top of the brownie was one firmly packed scoop of ice cream laying on the side. The scoop was a rich vanilla, flecked with dark specks of chocolate chips. The scoop of ice cream was draped with a rich, hot fudge sauce. Topping the luscious sauce was an ample splotch of whipped cream that was topped with a shower of finely chopped walnuts.

The contrast of colors, textures and flavors in this dessert appealed to every part of my senses. I could not wait to take a bite but it wasn't mine. A group of children were sharing the dessert, and the last thing I thought was to steal a group of students' dessert. What would they think?

Oh, this temptation had to stop, so I simply walked away from it and entered the staff's office to take my timetable. After doing that, I considered to freshen up in my room and keep my luggage.

## CHAPTER 7

# The School Bell

I was going through my timetable then slid it into the file. I saw Charlie from a distance and sauntered towards him.

I saw a big clock behind Charlie. It was built near the church. I remembered how schools would always have these big clocks denoting something significant. To my surprise the clock was not brown or copper in color. In fact, it was a mixture of bronze, copper and gold.

The big clock was built in a tower like building connected to the library. After a few minutes I heard the loud sound of the clock ticking and I saw that it was six pm.

I must check this out!

"How was the meeting with the principal?" asked Charlie with concern.

'Charlie thanks for asking. It went well and now I just want to rest my bones. I've had a pretty long journey.'

"Well, we are heading there, Ashley."

I stopped and saw a strange reptile passing by a tree near the apartment crawling towards the church.

The species looked rare and I was trying my best to remember what it was. I punched Charlie in the shoulder. 'Look at that. What is it? It's huge and heading to the church. Let's go and see it.'

Charlie's head bounced up and down. "Oh, yes, what is it? I will leave your luggage with the security."

My brisk walk depicted my eagerness to see the reptile. As I got closer it looked more like an Iguana. This Iguana look alike was turquoise in color with yellow and brown spots. The reptile did look strange. It was about a meter big and could probably weigh about sixty to seventy kilos, I assumed.

I was getting nervous and hoped not to be bitten by it. It looked so creepy. Without paying careful attention, I entered the orange colored door that led to the church. The reptile's movement paused and turned its head. I could see its grayish brown pair of eyes glaring at me and it continued crawling inside the church.

The curiosity was killing me. I didn't have much time to notice the interior of the church and simply followed the reptile. I could hear the school bell ringing and the sound began ascending louder and louder.

I was stunned to see the reptile instantly getting disoriented and a purple bubble like foam was erupting out of its system. There were purple bubbles in the air. There was a strange feeling of malevolence, as if a spiteful stare were fixed upon me. So, I took a few steps backwards.

I could not comprehend what was going on or what the hell it even was, until I noticed that my heart was palpitating, my hands were trembling and I was having goosebumps all over me. I was alone, and the sheer brutal horror of it overwhelmed me. My eyes strained against the complete and utter scenario left me speechless.

If I could name the reptile I would call it the 'Slimy Pudding.' From afar it looked just like a wobbly pudding. But the fact was it was a reptile. The eyes of the reptile were human like depicting a deep emotion or some kind of vengeance. It maneuvered its upright triangular ears to locate the faint rustling noises of shrews. I could not see any other than one that swiftly passed through. This was getting scary and I felt getting pulled towards it.

Taking steps ahead, the shrew was spread on top of fence against the far wall, its throat cut from ear to ear. Drops of blood fell from the fence with a drip-drip noise that sounded like a leaky faucet. It was disgusting. I felt something gush from my gut and into my throat. The food that was savored with delight came spewing out, covering the ground beneath me. The faintly feeling was something I never wanted to encounter again.

My eyes squinting, the swallowing of my saliva, taking deep breaths got me some air where I could distinguish the aroma of sanity from lunacy. I caught the balance of my mind and decided to discover what was happening. To my revelation no one was around me to witness anything I could see or went through.

"Ashley, where were you? The school bell has rung. It's time for an evening hymn for the students. We got to head to the assembly," spoke Charlie hastily.

When I turned around the strange looking reptile wasn't there but a puddle of red fluid was on the ground. It resembled a blood pool that left me speechless.

The school bell didn't stop and I felt that my head would explode. I looked up towards the dome like ceiling of the church and could see that the church's bell and school chorale were ringing and flowing simultaneously getting unpleasantly louder.

The sound was simply hideous to my observation. I felt I was taken on a wild ride wedged tightly between fear and insanity. Charlie was nowhere to be seen, he left. I could feel my feet wet, so I looked down and saw my feet inside the red fluid which slowly developed into a flood. The red fluid was rising inside the church and I slipped into it.

The thick fluid had risen three meters high that my effort to move forward to the exit was very difficult. Every attempt seemed like a failure. I dipped into the fluid closing my eyes.

Bubbles cascaded everywhere, racing one another to the surface. A shudder ran up my spine as I grew acclimatize to the new temperature. There was no sound milling around. Kicking my legs slowly I headed towards the exit. Without any warning, I fell flat on the marble floor. The red fluid simply evaporated leaving me there like a fool. My skin began to itch and I started to sniff. I howled in panic, writhing against the marble floor as if my hands and feet were handcuffed.

I tried to get out of the church gingerly. When I turned around I saw everything dry.

This was surely a torture and there was certainly something creepy trying to mess with me. I should leave this place, I believed.

I could feel my messy brown hair and slight freckles on my face covered with dust. I had placed my hand on my face and started brushing the dust out. I stood up and to my surprise I saw the reptile on top of the school bell.

I tried to speak, but my mouth was so dry with fear that I could only make soft wheezing noises.

I was perplexed and couldn't solve my confusion but simply stared at the school bell. By then the bell had stopped ringing.

I could hear a choir of students singing and the sound of the piano was melodious.

Nervously, I began twirling my brown hair around. The rope hanging under the school bell was getting longer and longer that it ultimately reached up to about twenty meters.

The white colored thick rope was just up to my reach. Clouds covered the moon, and the wind was whistling down the bell and rattling the shutters of the assembly hall. My eyes glowered with my mouth open. I simply bent down to take the rope in my hands and pulled the rope sideways.

The school bell began to ring again and I could hear peaceful sounds of paper turning. The crushing sounds of the moving leaves were buzzing around as if I was sitting beside a hive of bees scattered by a few louder statements.

I blinked my eyes and for a moment everything stopped and the rope slipped away from my fingers like someone pressed a rewind button. The sweat dripping down my face depicted the fear and puzzled situation I faced.

I took a deep breath and walked to get my luggage. I turned around to take a glance of the school bell.

The surprising act of nature or a message from an unknown source dived deep into my soul. The lights were dim, and seeing the fire crackling from a distance near the church got me to think deeply about my entrance to this new school.

I marveled with the fact that was this entrance a sign or symbol to exit or revenge taken by a supernatural source where the innocent was struggling with the beast.

This was indisputably a preview to a roller coaster ride.

## CHAPTER 8

# The Sandstorm

Sitting on the stairs for a while elevated my spirits. I was lethargic and my forehead was damp with sweat. I sat down for a while until I could figure out what I would do next.

"Ashley, where have you been? I have been finding you. You didn't turn up in the assembly. Don't tell me you were still in the church. Anyway, I have the keys to your room. Let me accompany you there." Charlie's facial muscles were tensed, and his anxious laughter escaped his lips.

'I'm sorry. I lost track of time. I would like to see the room and settle in. I need to organize my schedule so I won't miss anything important tomorrow,' I said anxiously.

Charlie helped me take my luggage and we went into the elevator. We got out on the sixth floor and walked towards room 606. The rooms were numbered strangely but I ignored it.

Charlie put in the key and opened the door. Walking in slowly into a small studio room, I put my hand bag on the high working table. I had thanked Charlie and he had briefed me about buying my necessities at the local supermarket behind the apartment.

He left the room and I began surveying the room carefully. I was impressed with the fact I had a small pantry where I could make a decent cup of coffee every morning. The table was near the pantry which could be used as a dining table and for work.

There was a long length bronze sequenced mirror next to the bookshelf. There was no TV, but there was free wireless connection. The room was cozy with a soft and comfortable sofa. The curtains were espresso and cream colored that balanced the room with a mixture of typical brown, cream, and peach colored interior.

The school and apartment seemed to have coordinated well with colors. I was glad that the room was not suffocating and decent enough for anyone to stay without feeling too homesick. I entered the bathroom and noticed the clean and well built restroom.

I began to unpack some stuff and took my file to go through it. Opening my laptop and getting connected with the wireless typing in the password given in the document got me relieved. I felt I was still in the normal world being connected to the internet, and wondering how two years would pass by after such a terror. I had to get out of this place somehow.

Going through the school map, flipping pages of the school policy book, and jotting down important things surely got time passing by until it was quite late.

I was hungry and could not find something I could nibble on. I wore my sweat pants and left to the supermarket.

Finding the supermarket wasn't hard and I bought various eatables to munch on. I remembered that I would be able to have breakfast, lunch, and tea at the canteen for free, but I couldn't resist buying Pringles and Diet Coke.

I placed everything in the pantry feeling at home then went for a shower.

The shower was amazing after a long ass day. I was quite calm and didn't recall the incident that happened. It was more like as if I was in denial and simply went with the flow. Spraying the cinnamon and chamomile aroma therapy pillow mist, I felt quiet relaxed and dosed off to sleep.

It was a fresh new day. I could see an acre of grass and gardens around the church from my window pane. I drew the curtains and opened the window. Two crows pecked in the grass looking for worms. I quickly sipped my coffee and took a shower.

I did not want to be late because I wanted to see the entire school today. That was my aim.

I dressed up professionally and elegantly with my black leather suit jacket.

Pacing toward the canteen I stopped by an empty classroom. An antique metallic sculpture of a young girl kept in the middle of two book shelves caught my attention. The sculpture was amazing with the well carved blend of bronze, gold, yellow, silver, and brown colored metal. The young girl was holding a torch and tiptoed as if she was in the middle of doing something. The expression of the sculpture denoted loneliness. It seemed that the naked pity in peoples' eyes made her want to shout, "Go away! I don't yearn for your sympathy."

I touched the smooth metallic carving and said, 'Excellent piece of art.'

The human like statuette showed a creative spirit and skill that exhibited good balance, and craftsmanship. I turned around and saw the well equipped room for grade six.

I saw the clock, and quickly left to the canteen.

Various types of cuisines were available that got me quite excited with seeing different counters.

I took a cup of coffee and scooped a range of salad leaves on my plate. While taking a croissant and bagel, I saw a man from a distance. He was chatting with some students. His lightening grin was irresistibly devastating to my calm reserve. I beamed at his charming enthusiasm towards the children.

I sat down and ate my breakfast. From a distance Elma noticed me sitting alone and joined me. We were chatting casually and she briefed me about different teachers in the campus.

The bell had rung and we dispersed. Elma had a class while I was loitering around the campus to get familiar with.

The urge of going to the bathroom distracted Elma and she couldn't wait any longer. She had assigned some work and walked out of the class.

When she was pacing toward the bathroom she saw me.

"Hey, Ashley!"

I wheeled around and saw Elma waving at me. She walked towards me quickly and I asked, 'What's up! Is there . . .'

"I really need to use the bathroom. Please see to my class for a couple of minutes. I have assigned them some work. Thanks."

'Sure Elma.'

I entered the classroom and saw the students doing their work. They were drawing a fish and labeling it.

I skimmed through the classroom and walked around to see the way some students were drawing. Praising some of them with their creative skills, I turned and paused.

Completely stunned and stared at the sculpture I had seen a few hours ago. I was actually back in the same room. I went ahead and looked at it again.

The sculpture of the young girl surely depicted African heritage in several ways such as, fertility, rain, natural calamities, or even evil spirits. Glancing at every detail, I assumed it was built more than thirty to forty years ago. The torch in her hand had an ivory tinted stone around it. It simply looked intricate and classic. The graceful and powerful sculpture denoted something special that I was trying to figure out.

The piece of artistic cultivation reflected some positive notion. Letting out a sigh, I turned and strolled toward the desk. I recognized and remembered that I was inside the class of grade six after I saw a label of some science materials on the shelf.

I sat down on the tip of the desk noticing some dust particles on the table. Taking a closer look, I noticed that the dust looked like sand particles. My brow raised, and felt my nose creasing as I was touching the particles and smeared it on my palm.

It was quite unusual and I marveled with curiosity. I could hear an echo of someone calling my name as if it was a young girl whispering. "Ashley."

This can't be The Mummy game; I wondered and frowned with worry.

The noise rose higher and higher, and the sculpture pulsed with a strident yellow light that smote my eyes, making them water.

I sensed a shiver through my body. My fingers were trembling and some dust particles were on my nails.

I tilted to take a glance at the students, slowly and gradually the room was getting dustier and the students couldn't be seen. The yellowish brown colored sand had engulfed in the air making my eyes itch. It started getting sandier and windy. I began pushing against the raging wind. I couldn't believe what was happening. The twirls of sand movement embraced me with it making me twirl around in fast movements. Pain oozed from my joints and sweat trickled down my spine.

The students were nowhere. Everything seemed like an illusion. I could not breathe feeling suffocated.

I dropped flat on the floor next to the desks. My fast eye movements and hands covering my eyes signaled a yearning to be rescued. I heard my name being called several times, but couldn't distinguish where it came from. A soft voice of a young girl called out my name very persistently, "Ashley Preston . . ."

'Am I a laughing stock here? Who the hell is it?' I screamed with frustration.

The continuous flow of echo was stagnant and didn't raise any tone while calling out my name.

A blast of wind and sand rose up through the musty air. Sand was in my eyes and my vision was blurry but I could just make out a distant shadow approaching. It was certainly a shadow of the young girl.

My eyes rolled up, 'Who are you? This is not The Mummy game, alright. Stop-stop! I repeated several times.'

My face went blank and confused. I closed my eyes and was lying on my back on the floor flapping and rolling my legs up in the air.

The scene was quite hilarious for the students as I heard them burst into laughter. The giggles of them were pounding in my ears.

"What's going on, Ashley?" asked Elma curiously.

With a frown, I continued hastily, "I know I took a little more time, and you made a mess out here. You are acting like a duck. What's up?"

Hearing to the words of Elma, I squinted and looked sideways. The room was absolutely sand free. Not a speck of dust was anywhere. I swallowed my saliva, 'I am sorry. I guess just a trick of creativity . . . I know I am making no sense. Glad you arrived,' I said in hesitance.

A flash of humor crossed my face depicting warmth and generosity.

Elma chuckled and the teasing laughter was back in her eyes.

I tittered, covering my mouth, 'Crazy day . . . I shall get going. But before that, could I take a look at the room? I won't be loud. The sculptures are quite interesting.'

I sounded like nothing even happened and managed to stand still. Surveying the room, my eyes met a broken ivory piece. I took it and slipped it into my pocket.

Something was definitely not right here. A sandstorm in the class was surely pathetic, yet created an intense drama in my life. I walked toward the sculpture of the young girl and saw it was perfectly flawless. I changed my mind when I saw a few sand particles in the corner of the eyes of the figure.

I shuffled my feet in the silent room, without disturbing the students; I brushed out the sand particles. My right hand began trembling when I could feel a soft flesh of skin on the figure, as though it was the cheek of a soft baby.

My eyes met the eyes of the sculpture and I felt pulled towards it. I moved her hand and the innocent looking figure winked at me.

I took a step backward, that doesn't make sense. Now I feel like a lunatic, I muttered. My brows wrinkled, and my lips flattened together. 'What the f . . .'

I turned around, simply waved at Elma and stormed out of the room. Standing in the passage way for a few minutes got me able to think straight for a while. I lifted my arms and saw that I was dust free. This can't be a delusion. I am not a freak. Something is certainly crazy here. I got to find out the history of this school or I better tell Principal Orchestra and get out of this haunted place.

From the way Principal Orchestra spoke to me on the first day, her sarcasm seemed to conceal a dark story, I presumed.

If Edwin ever heard this he would laugh at me and remind me of all the superstitious crap. This place could be cursed by voodoo? Or if this doesn't stop I got to have a word with the Principal, I considered.

# CHAPTER 9

# The Signature

Peace, Peace, Peace . . . was ringing in my mind. I needed a quiet place to think, so I ambled towards the library. I wanted to sit inside for a while to get my mind sorted out of the bumpy ride I had gone through.

I entered the library and went up to the second floor. The library looked amazing with its antique architecture taking one to the Victorian era. If one dug a little deeper beneath the established architecture there was valuable history of tales that were ready to be revealed, and one could find something that would be totally captivating and maneuvering.

I felt my thoughts were straddling the conspiracy between illusion and reality. I did not want to turn insane. I wanted to be just the way I was when I came here—Normal!

Taking a deep breath I got up and began going through a pile of books on the table diagonal to mine.

I flipped pages of various books and noticed that in one of the books there was a scribble of a student. I assumed it was just another mischievous act, but when the pages began flipping without any effort, I believed that there was no place tailor-made for the mystery and masquerading in HAVEN. Something was definitely up and I was ready to hunt for the inscrutability the incidents were trying to hint.

On the side of the book, there was a signature of a student by the name of *Sarah Compton*. Hmm . . . it must be one the impish ones, I wonder with disappointment.

The signature could illustrate something about this person I wonder. Perhaps a graphologist could describe the personality or when this person had signed on the book. A debate was taking place in my mind where I wanted to know more about the person's handwriting. It could portray something or probably nothing. Was it even worth an attempt?

I closed the book with fear and considered going to my apartment where I could take a nap so I could feel fresh for lunch. I was in no mood to explore neither the school nor the library at this point.

Striding out of the library and passing by some classrooms, I appreciated the fresh breeze. I walked towards the supermarket and could see a playing ground from a distance. While I was heading there, I could hear the sound of water flowing.

I turned around and saw a small artificially built waterfall.

This is great. I am checking this out. The library did not make me feel better but got me into another track of analyzing a signature, I wondered.

I walked towards the waterfall and noticed a few benches scattered around the area where I could take the pleasure in the artificially built forest like spot. It was spectacular.

Sitting down under the shade where the tree branches were branching out like an umbrella was soothing. I felt sleep deprived and the incidents I had gone through were certainly now a challenge I faced to solve. My fingers bent were touching my chin and my half shut eyes depicted calmness and a moment of respite.

It would be a worthy joy defeating an opponent. If there was certainly something going on, I am ready to annihilate the tricks the evil or whatever it is completely.

The mild blend of the fragrance of grass and flowers around the waterfall developed a feeling where I felt I was transported into a world of fantasy and wondered that will the tug of war expose what lies on the other side of the path of bewilderment.

After having sat for a while, I left to my apartment. Walking gingerly and inhaling the fresh air was comforting.

Taking out the key from my blue leathered handbag, I inserted it to the keyhole and twirled the knob.

The reflection of the sun's rays on the bed divulged its quiet melancholic beauty. I placed my bag on the table and flipped off my shoes. I simply opened my arms and fell flat on the bed allowing no effort to stop but with lightness I devoted an hour for an extravagant power nap.

The power nap enveloped me into a soulful happiness where I could dive into a world where no incidents would drag me into an unwanted performance of drama.

Time had granted a calm and voluntary act where one could sleep though all negativity only if time was not challenged by a persona of a powerful spirit.

I believe I was in deep sleep, until I could hear a hazy sound of the splashing waters that created a steady pattern of endless rhythm. I twisted and felt disturbed by the sound. The roars of water started to get louder and louder.

I tried to take the other pillow to cover my ears but couldn't as my eyes gave a hard and unblinking stare. I quickly got out of the bed, falling down on the floor pulling my blanket with me.

I was rubbing my eyes with small fists, 'Who are you? When did you get into my room? I can't even get a decent sleep. This place is crazy,' I grumbled with frustration.

She was a young girl lying on my bed. She turned and placed her elbow on the pillow sticking out her tongue.

I could feel a prickling sensation at the back of my neck as if someone was poking the cactus leaves leaving me stinging. With a sudden jerk I could feel the sensation subside until I heard a soft voice.

"Ahem . . . ahem, this won't take long since I have already introduced myself to you with the grand presence of the sand storm. My name is *Sarah Compton*. I would like to be precise and didn't find the need to show you more tricks since you had seen enough."

'Uhmm . . . You created the sandstorm. Okay, you're not a ghost or something, right? It could simply be some voodoo or some sort of a magical trick,' I stated hastily. Swallowing my saliva I broke into a panic run. 'Oh Lord! What the hell! A spirit on my bed, I am losing my mind.' It felt as I was snapped awake out of a deep sleep, and began screaming aloud in horror.

Rubbing around her nose, "You saw what you saw. I am not a ghost but a spirit with a precious proposal for you. Before I go down memory lane, and hear your excuses which are simply going to disturb my ears, I shall tell you that you have no choice.

Stop screaming! I have been waiting for someone who is simply going to release me and my friend Thomas from this place," said Sarah with her convincing voice.

'Oh Shit! Sh-i-t . . .'

"No swearing, Ashley. It doesn't suit a teacher like you," said Sarah with sarcasm.

The muscles in her forehead were constricting, her brows wrinkled, and my lips flattened together, 'Okay, let me breathe. Was this a scene from some fiction movie? Why do I feel I am reliving the moment for some comedy thriller. Seriously, stop joking and your friend Thomas, tell him to stop playing this hide and seek game. It's time you guys get out of here. You dorks would simply kill me. You can't be in the teacher's room. Get out and I certainly didn't like this prank. Next time think of something better,' I said pointing my finger at her.

Sarah got up and smiled at me. She winked and blew a flying kiss at me. In the shape of a kiss, steam like smoke had engulfed the room and a young boy was sitting on the lamp next to the window pane.

'Ahhhh . . . . this is not a magic or witch school. Is it?' I stammered furiously.

I looked at Thomas, the corner of his mouth drooped like a puppy.

"It was so funny to see you scared and more than that someone can see us, Sarah. We have found her, finally. Nice to meet you, my name is *Thomas Boyle*. Yeah, yeah . . . we are spirits and you are going to be our source of help. There are no guarantees of success and your inquisitive thoughts are crowning over our plight where in time your questions will be answered after you hear our story."

Watching the ghostly figures slip through my room, my mind was now manipulating my behavior. It was strange. I wanted to cry out for help.

Could I text someone: *SOS! Ghosts!*

Who would come? No one, I need help. Someone—SOS

My doubt to come to teach was unquestionably a bad choice. This was no salvation, but more like someone strangling my neck to slowly stop the easy navigation of oxygen into my system.

I thought slavery was over. Now I shall become a slave of these GHOSTS. Oh no . . . this is not happening.

Taking a deep breath, I went to grab a glass of water. I sat down on my sofa and noticed that Thomas and Sarah just looked at me innocently.

They were watching every move and listening to every word I said out of frustration and fear.

'Fine, tell me your story and I know I can't escape so I will be a good listener and not sleep. This better be good. This is certainly not a two friendly spirits meeting time in my bedroom and I presume you guys are about thirteen or fourteen years old. Damn . . . shoot,' I said restlessly.

The spirits were shaped like a misty cloud where a clear depiction of a person did show but one could not feel his or her skin.

It started to get hot and Sarah's skin was peeling.

I feel my mouth dry and heart beat increasing.

"You have seen various tricks since you have arrived and you know what we are capable of. Each of us has a wish. This is a trade, our wish is fulfilled and you return back to Hawaii or else you never see or feel the fresh air again. Every day you will be drowned with displeasures which will be worse than your break up," said Sarah mordantly.

I was shocked and the glass of water slipped off my fingers. The pieces of glass were the proof that they were not lying and were here for a reason.

I began to weep and wiping my tears that were trickling down my face. I sniffed, 'You are an encyclopedia and surely know many things about me. I don't want to get this messy. I have a life too. Let's be fair and let me do my job and perhaps you can be my part-time hobby. You are like this child who is simply so stubborn and will not stop until she gets her lollipop.'

"I am not a child who is stubborn. I am a sixteen year old who is here for revenge from life as it deceived me," said the rebellious Thomas and shook his fist in the air.

"We are not going to plead, but we know only you can help us with your expertise and there is nothing you can do to escape. I am fifteen years old and did die very young. We will see you again and leave you to your power nap," said Sarah as she flipped her messy hair.

Thomas and Sarah faded away and simply disappeared as if they were some sort of steam.

The magnificent imperial of thoughts shattered when I knew she was there for a purpose and when I had accepted the challenge in the library, I should have known they were watching. How creepy can this get?

Instantly, I recalled the name Sarah Compton from one of the books. My lips were compressed and my heartbeat was getting faster and louder. I could feel my pressure getting low. I was pressing my neck to ease out the stress.

I picked up the broken pieces of glass and threw it into the trash can. I got myself back on the bed trying to feel comfortable again. But it was hard!

Later I stood up, this time I saw from the window pane that two pigeons were patrolling the dusty cement path.

It felt like the conniving destiny had raised more secrets that offered a platter of spirits instead of something relishing. It was hard to escape the perplexity which had already become an addiction creating an obsession where I was merely a puppet and the string puller were ghosts who took the pleasure of every act.

Will the next series of acts be reviving or would it simply end me up like one of them too?

I went to sleep with pondering notions of various stories I could think of as these kids had cultivated a new branch making my life more complex and melodramatic.

I guess the countdown had begun to solve a new mystery or who knows a misery.

## CHAPTER 10

# Incurable Mining

Brushing off the dust from the sofa, I then placed my towel on it. I put on some gloss and was ready to leave back to school. I didn't want to miss the evening tea and hymn this time because of some ridiculous magic trick by desperate spirits. I had to trust my imagination to suggest a way for me to settle the conflict affably.

Time was not to tell what would happen next as I had to decide that this time I would control time and destroy the act of catastrophic drama. I didn't need any of this bamboozlement but something had to happen to further solidify my beliefs.

Walking down the passageway of the school surrounded by shimmering lights was just like a bride walking down an aisle surrounded by floras and various chic décor welcoming a new beginning.

I felt welcomed but by the honorable spirits. I turned around to see if they were following me and were up to any bizarre actions. But I saw no one, so I continued walking.

"Hey. How are you feeling? You really seemed out of your mind before, Ashley?" asked Elma and waved at Zuri.

Zuri paced towards them and was introduced to Ashley.

Elma continued, "Ashley, it's important you get familiar with everyone around you, even though he is a janitor. He has been working for us for many years and sings quite well. See him join the other kids at the assembly. He does it every week."

Zuri smiled slightly and took permission to leave.

They had head to the canteen for a cup of tea. The guilt and embarrassment of what had happened at class was bugging me. I preferred to speak less and pay attention more at every move as I knew I was being watched at all times.

Having taking a cup of White Tea mixed with Chamomile and with some slices of butter cake, I sat down on the bench.

I looked around the canteen suspiciously and spotted the man I saw during breakfast. He was taking a sandwich and walked towards me. I did not know what to do so I took out my phone from my handbag and flipped the phone open pretending to use it.

But he did not sit with me and sat behind on the other table. I heard Elma greet him and invited him to sit with us.

He declined the offer politely and she came to sit with me.

Her mouth widened, "You should meet Dominic. He is quite amiable and conservative at the same time."

'Who is he? Are you talking about the person behind us? Do I have to know him too?' I asked with apprehension.

"Come on, you should know all the teachers' here pretty much. Maybe later after tea or the assembly I will introduce you guys. Who knows the day is inviting you to explore all the areas of existence that involve a strong expression of feeling, a declaration of love, a spiritual confession, and all these kinds of communication might bring into the light a kind of intimate revelation," said Elma dramatically.

Eyebrow was raised and nose wrinkled, 'Wait a minute, Love! Are you in love? I didn't know you had this side of you too. Hmm . . . so you like this guy, yeah.'

"Nah, it was some sort of parody for you. May be you and him, you know what I mean," teased Elma and winked.

'Of course not, a fit of gloom has descended upon me, as if responsibilities of the moment have been way too much for me. I shall rather step out and be the observer. I shall maintain the professional relationship here rather than any intimacy nonsense,' I said with a smile.

I sipped my tea and took a bite of the cake. In my moment of silence I began wondering about this man who was claimed to be appealing and mind grabbing.

The bell had rung and everyone was getting ready to go to the assembly. The evening hymn and parade of an army of students' and teachers' made the scene look quite motivating.

I sat in the front row next to Elma and a few seconds later, Dominic sat next to me. I glanced at him and quickly lost focus because he was handsome to be a teacher. Or let's say Teachers can be handsome. What am I thinking? Well looks deceive I remembered and chose to listen to the chorus of singers.

I saw Zuri sing along at the famous and one of my favorite *Alleluia! Alleluia!* It was harmonious. I was quite impressed and had underestimated the talent of everyone.

Elma turned and winked at me signaling about Dominic, but I lowered my eyes and wished I could hide. I simply showed no interest at all. My response to the situation felt like I was a high school girl again.

'Calm down Ashley, you have no time for love since you have a special case on spirit tragedy to solve,' said the sarcastic soul from within.

These words echoed in my mind. I watched the choir attentively and ignored any distractions.

The evening hymn was over and Principal Orchestra said a few words before everyone was dismissed. She sounded cold.

On the way out, Elma introduced Dominic as *Dominic Thurston* to me. We initiated a conversation with a plainspoken voice and headed to the staff room.

I was introduced to everyone formally by Elma and was asked some questions by some teachers to get familiar with.

Dominic joined us on the table where I was seated. I could tell that he was gazing at me as I was going through my timetable and circling something.

I smiled at him, 'My first class, starts tomorrow. It's quite thrilling. So what grade do you teach again?'

He shook his head, "I am sure it would be exhilarating. I teach the secondary level Physics and Chemistry. You do have a strong American accent."

'Oh yes. And—you sure do have a typical accent of an Australian which I am trying to get familiar with,' I teased.

When I titled my head, I saw Elma look at us and seemed glad I had probably made a new friend.

I excused myself and went to the toilet. While I walked out, I hinted Elma that we needed to talk. She got up and excused for the same reason.

"Ashley, what's wrong? I was simply trying to be friendly and I am not interested in Dominic because I am already engaged to a Turkish business owner for two years. After my contract I am going to get married. Take it easy and go with a flow. You look as if you are constipated," said Emily her tone castigating.

'That was a nice pep talk! I am going with a flow and I don't look constipated, okay. Just need time adjusting with this whole new series of activities I have been drawn into. And please don't tease me about this guy again. We are not in high school,' I expressed sarcastically.

The sun had set and everyone had dispersed to embrace the space they got and do whatever they wanted. I felt relieved that I did not have to face anything silly and continued to stride towards my apartment.

I was feeling famished and was looking forward to cook noodles and watch my series that had been downloaded by now.

While I was walking, I could hear flies buzzing and it was getting irritating with the annoying sound. I looked up and was stunned to see Sarah and Thomas shaped like Fireflies.

'Oh, no! Seriously! Fine, that was creative . . . umm . . . shit . . . I see your faces and your body glows.'

"So, someone did not scream and is beginning to face us. Your level of courage and determination is very high, and you have the ability to accomplish unusual achievements," said Thomas and buzzed close to my ears.

'Look, I cannot scream here. I feel like I am going to pee in my pants. Are you joining me to have noodles or you would be kind enough for me to sleep peacefully tonight, since I have my first class tomorrow?'I responded crisply.

Sarah watched disbelievingly and there was an involuntary cry that left her lips.

'Stop it and just buzz or fly somewhere else,' I waved my hand in the air to shoo them away. But that didn't help. They simply flew around me until I was more infuriated.

To my surprise, Dominic stood on the other side of the floor and watched me wave my hand continuously and looked rather bugged.

"What's wrong?"

'Ahh . . . flies. I hate them.'

Sarah and Thomas were flying in circles on top of Dominic's head.

I was distracted by them that I tripped.

"So we stay on the same floor, Ashley. I am in room 601 on the other side."

'Yes, I guess so . . . 606, is where I stay. I got to leave. See you tomorrow,' I spoke and took off briskly.

He does have this awkward charm when he looks at me. Oh Lord, he can't be a temptation. I should avoid. Awkward! Awkward! I repeat continuously inwardly.

Dominic could probably make out that I looked disturbed. He possibly thinks it was because of some flies and finds me strange as I just ambled to my room, I thought.

I opened the door and banged it close. I counted one to ten, 'No time to get pissed. I need to cook noodles and switch on some music.'

Sarah and Thomas were staring at me and enjoyed seeing me bugged. Instead, Sarah sat on the bookshelf and lifted her hand as if she was the Pope and Thomas was sitting with his legs crossed observing me.

"Is it us or Dominic, you are petrified with?" asked Thomas with a wink.

I gestured him to zip his mouth and leave me alone.

The Fireflies did brighten the room with more chaos and were not there to leave but become an unwanted companion to stir up the moment with more drama.

I made my noodles, took a shower and wore my pajamas. I couldn't be bothered as I knew my privacy was invaded until I was released from the prison where the jailors were two spirits.

While eating noodles and sipping Iced Lemon Tea, the Fireflies had a great watch on me. Then they flew towards me and rested next to where I had placed my laptop.

'You kidding me!'

With every muscle tense, I heard the chiming of falling glass from a broken window, and the gnarring sound of a nose pressed to the floor.

'I am going to watch Downton Abbey and you two are simply fishing around here,' I blurted out.

I love Downton Abbey as it would take me to a remarkable era where I was simply dazzled. The series was marvelous and a pull towards another world.

"Look who is so drawn to something that is fiction. If you like this, you will like my story. It's nonfiction with an astonishing twist. You wanna hear . . ." interrupted Sarah.

I could hear the click-clicking of her nails. The musky, foul smell of her hair combined with the brawny breath of an animal, drifted into the room.

'Shoosh—you stinky!'

She wasn't a shadowy spirit as I could place my finger on her lips indicating a signal to shut up.

With a toss of his flashy tummy Thomas said, "I see your point, but you got to hear this. I request you. I don't usually do that . . . or else . . ."

'I forgot that I simply live in your world now. I don't even know how humans live anymore. Now my entertainment every night would be Fireflies or God knows what you come as next time. Oh, you dead teenagers are so getting on my nerves. Okay go on . . . go on.'

Faster, faster, I commanded my hands, panting desperately against the fear choking. Being surrounded by dead people was out of my reach. My spirit to fight against them was buried under the marshy land of fright.

I pressed the pause icon and pointed at Sarah to start her tale of twist. Sarah was anxious and cleared her throat before she started. The dark secret and the tale that would change my life was about to begin. So far I had just seen a preview. The actual movie was yet to begin, I marveled.

"I am going to tell you a life of some miners. This goes back forty-five years when this school was near a diamond mining field and technology was still on an introduction stage. I belonged to a family where women were miners and the men were simply beastly. All they wanted was to depend on women and live a pleasantly lazy life. Not all men were like that, but the family I came from was messy. I went to school like some kids and was then forced into child labor. That was when I couldn't finish school," expressed Sarah.

Thomas was buzzing around and dancing with awkward movements creating a light hearted scenario, it didn't work, so I tried spraying insecticide on him but ended up sneezing.

Sarah smacked Thomas on his cheeks, "You will have your turn, too."

She continued, "The school I studied in was quite small and this town was practically segmented in small areas which separated many types of people. My mother was American and my father was African. They met during work and had gotten married. Mom had chosen to be one of the few Americans who would be a diamond miner in Africa. I was the only child and knew nothing much about mining. The late 1960's did not do any justice to child labor and you may even be going against theories. You were not even born, so you would not be troubled by this rebelliousness as much I was."

Sarah's was slowly changing and reformed to a young girl. She was no longer a Firefly. Her hair glints burnished copper and red under the lamplight.

I stopped eating and saw the real her. She was dusky with brown eyes. She had shouldered hair which was curly and clipped all over. Her chubby body depicted a cute teenager growing through her adolescence.

The formation and change from a fly to a young girl made me antsy. 'Then what went wrong?' I asked and put down my bowl of noodles.

Sarah had undergone a dynamic change and she sat closer to me, while Thomas was resting his small butt on top of the edge of the spoon.

"One day, with an unexpected mudslide I was trapped inside the mine with some women. I cried out for help but nothing worked nor did anyone come for our rescue. The entire slope collapsed and I was dead just like that. SNAP. I wondered trying to figure out what happened and saw my parents feel the guilt as they couldn't fight against child labor. Their tears were an ocean of pain within," said Sarah and her tears welled in her eyes.

She wept for some time until she started snorting. The strange sound and her pain got the environment in the room humid. A strange smell started to diffuse around the room as if it was a room filled with dead people.

The peculiar sour and stale smell aggravated a queasy feeling. I took my air freshener and sprayed it several times but the odor got stronger. The battle between two smells instigated a war of reality and the unwanted death of a young teenager.

'Please stop! Please stop!' I shouted.

Sarah slowly stopped weeping and the odd smell in the room started to subside. "Can you even imagine what I went through? I was trapped. My body rotted, and the sanitation was absolutely nil for people like us. What did I do to deserve that? There is no difference between my dusky skin and mud or even sand. I was buried with mud and grinded completely as death embraced me," complained Sarah.

A stray breeze swept through the room with a murmur: "Revenge! Revenge! Revenge!"

I couldn't answer right away. Angst and fright had stilled my tongue. I couldn't imagine what she went through. Sarah's twist of tale did rekindle my keenness to solve the mystery of her wondering around.

'So, what do you want now? It is sad and nothing can change the fact that the mudslide had to appear . . . and . . .'

I paused mid-sentence and stared in shock as she laughed and began to change. Her body twisted and broke before my eyes repeating the words—"Revenge! Revenge! Revenge!"

"Well, I am back to finish this story," disrupted Sarah.

'What do you mean? Do want to this school to undergo a mudslide just because you went through it. That is crazy,' I added with worry.

"No, this is a task that only you can accomplish because it is your job. For a strange reason, I want to complete my high school diploma. I want to experience livelihood of high school," yelled Sarah.

I stood up and took a deep breath, 'So you want me to enroll you to my class with the rest of the students who are alive and you realize that this wouldn't be possible, right?'

Sarah's eyes was getting red and she was biting her teeth, "Exactly, you got to do that. I just want that! Release me forever.

I am still stuck in the mudslide and if you don't figure out how this is done, you shall surely see one yourself."

'It's not like a person enters a room and introduces a class that we have a new student, guess what—she is dead, a ghost and has come all the way from the 1960s to attain a school diploma. You realize that your presence has a powerful impact on the people around you, so don't take things lightly. It's not like I am a queen giving a proclamation to my kingdom. You have to make sure that you do not harm anyone and I got to sort this out,' I explained with fear.

I took a piece of paper and jotted down the names of Sarah and Thomas. On the side I had put a star next to it. I noted what Sarah demanded and kept the paper on the table.

Sarah was quiet, but her look was certainly messy and quite direct with what she wanted. Her story was aspiring as she had the hope to feel that she would be released for sure and waited for the right moment.

Mining was fraught and dangerous, and the possibility of collapsing walls and drowning simply flipped me to a next chapter. I was now on a mission to help a spirit get a high school diploma after forty-five years.

Seriously! That was pathetic. I must call Edwin. He would freak, too. His take on spirits was certainly in my face. Could he see spirits? I wonder with that strange curiosity.

I looked at Thomas wearily and knew he wanted the same. I was silent and waited to listen to his story.

Sarah's witty nature and keen mental awareness was providing me with accidental opportunities to jump into a flame of desired dreams which I was still yet to encounter.

My appetite was flushed with the thirst of revenge and foul smell.

# CHAPTER 11

# The Dignified Slave

Thomas was lying down on the spoon and was rather drowsy. The deep worry line between my eyes got me thinking what story would take place next.

Yawning away, "This would be your new bed time story," mocked Thomas.

I glowered, 'Why don't you just speak. I need to sleep too.'

Thomas's corners of his mouth quirked upward. His cheeky smile was ready to expose another dark story.

He scratched his forehead, "As Sarah mentioned, 1960s was probably an era for a transition for the world and slavery had ended for many but for a few it seemed like life was too cheap. My parents still fought the battle for a better life. We waited for the dawn for a normal life; it felt life had been given to a pawn shop. In return we only got a chance to breathe freely and nothing else."

"The rich beat us in law and if that didn't work they would burn us off our land. Other villagers looked around and said we could have a ceasefire, but we knew we would lose no matter what. It was better to give in," he added.

His eyebrows furrowed, and his lips pressed together. His face was turning red. I didn't take him seriously, I found it rather hilarious as she saw his face turning red and his body was glowing.

He clenched his hands, "I used to go to school a few days a week and I had to help collect stuff from the sewage plant daily. As a child I wanted to run away and kill those landlords who tortured my family. Because of them, my cousin's right leg got crooked. She hobbled lopsidedly for a short distance, and then had to rest all the time. This is no typical story but one of the facts of history. This chapter of life on hidden slavery did not end. The exploitation was simply ridiculous. Fate betrayed me."

He transformed his body into a chair. It looked quite strange that he looked exactly like an antique wooden chair and was rocking back and forth. Only his face could be seen.

"We were never part of slavery. My father was part of the navy and came to Africa to help but rather got trapped by a few greedy people who were Blacks. The political game forced him to be a slave and my mom helped me collecting things daily. She then returned home and used to cook a meal for us. My father couldn't go anywhere and visited us once in a few months. He protected us and wanted to keep us away from the terror he knew would spread like plague," described Thomas.

I felt I was watching a History Channel and was taken to the past. I got up and kept my bowl in the sink and placed my pillow upright so I could lean on it.

When Thomas saw I got myself comfortable he continued, "I still remember that day when father came to visit us. He had mentioned how he was stranded and was escorted directly only to meet us for the day and had to return back late evening. We lived in a small village where human rights were still in progress. The suffocation instigated a rescue plan. He was planning to escape but it was getting too difficult to do anything. That day while he was chatting with us, we heard an explosion. Some Blacks and British people were fighting against some people who simply took advantage of the whole system. No one could tell who was supporting who since a mixture of people where fighting against the wrong. There were reporters covering the scene and many people were hurt. That was the best time to escape. We did exactly that."

Thomas shivered and the chair collapsed. He changed his form to young British boy. He sat next to me on the bed. I got off the bed and sat on the sofa. I didn't want to sit next to him.

Sheer terror made him suddenly valiant. He sulked.

Sarah was noticing every move that she giggled on how I reacted. She took the Pringles box and wanted to taste the classic chips.

My eyes widened as I saw Sarah eat her chips. The crunching sound was annoying.

I glanced at Thomas and pointed my index finger towards him to continue talking.

Thomas had a smirk, "We were forced to live in Africa after my dad was captured and forced to serve a rich Black man because he was seeking vengeance. My dad will always be a hero. He had planned to return back to England. Mom had packed the necessary belongings and she held my hand tightly as we left the brick home. I saw that someone had shaved off another person's black hair to the scalp and stubbed out cigarettes on his arms. I was so nervous and scared. I didn't want to face that. We ran and had passed through a sewage canal. We had seen a bloated body floating. The scene was terrifying and we had to walk quickly. From a distance we saw a group of people running towards us. We had to disperse. Mom and I ran until I came quite in front and jumped into a canal strewn with rubbish. I could see from afar that some people were being hit. I hid deep and was throttled with the dreadful smell."

I knew this was getting intense and somehow Thomas did go through hell where he couldn't feel the justice and nothing made any sense to this boy.

Sarah stretched out her bony hands toward Thomas's shaking body offering him some Pringles.

My teary eyes symbolized sympathy for the children and I knew I could only listen. To cheer them up I asked, 'Do you guys want ice cream? Can you guys eat ice cream? I can see one eating chips so the other could probably have ice cream.'

"Yes, we can eat anything. We have the ability to," interrupted Sarah.

Smiling tentatively, "I don't mind it. Would like to taste it," said Thomas with hesitance.

'Umm . . . you guys are spirits then how could you eat? This is all getting bizarre and quite difficult to understand. Here you go, try the chocolate biscuit. There is vanilla ice cream between the chocolate cookies. I shall have one too,' I say as I open the wrapper.

Thomas didn't open the wrapper but rather swallowed the entire ice cream with the plastic wrapper. Sarah followed me and was acting to be sophisticated.

He blinked his eyes, "This was cooling and I liked it. So, I was in the rubbish for hours. I could feel my skin swollen and bloated. My head was hurting so bad that I couldn't breathe. I coughed several times and tried to lift myself up but couldn't. I cried then howled but nothing worked. I could feel my eyes widened and the upper lids rose, depicting my fear. I couldn't even remember when I stopped breathing. When I woke up, I rushed out of the rubbish and tried finding my parents but I couldn't. They were nowhere to be found."

He took the other pillow and stretched it in anger. He glared at me with depth. His jaw had thrust forward and the lips pressed together. His tears were trickling down his eyes slowly increasing speed that the room began to flood.

I tilted downward and saw my feet wet. I couldn't believe what was going on and how I would get the room clean. The color of the water was brownish black as if it was from a sewage canal. I quickly rose my feet, 'Please, stop it Thomas! My room can't be changed into a sewage dump. You got to get hold of yourself and get to the point.'

My hands were trembling with nervousness. I tried to console him and did agonize with his pain. Eventually he calmed down by blowing up the windows. A loud thud and the shattering glass added more drama to the scene.

Thomas stretched his hand and placed his fingers on the table. He began tapping on it, "I wish I could see my parents for the last time, but atleast want to know what happened to them. I know they are in England. One more thing, I have never ever gone on a date. I want to experience that."

The water had cleared out from the room and everything was dry. I was surprised with what Thomas asked for.

A ghost came back because he wanted to go out on a date. He smells worst than pee and any girl would rather die than go out on a date with a stinky person. How unromantic and wretched this would get, I contemplated.

Flipping my hair, 'Do you even think this makes sense? You want to date a person alive and you are so sure that she would take you in her arms loving every moment. You know you smell horrible—big time. More than that, you're dead. Are you crazy?'

"I am not crazy, but what a high school boy would want anything more that experience his first date. I shall choose and you got to behave like a wing man or woman," stated Thomas enthusiastically.

Sarah clapped a couple of times continuously, "So, now you have a project to complete and release us."

Rubbing around my ear, 'So, I see there is no point going on a debate. Thomas, about your family, it's a long time now, your parents might be dead now. Let's see what I can find out only if I am free, and about your date there is no need to dream too much. It is ridiculous, but I shall see what can be done. Sarah, you need to start attending classes, or who knows you already might be doing that since both of you have been here for a long time. I haven't even started teaching real students and I got to think about dead people. This is insane . . . I am sorry both of you did go through something no one should. However, this can't be changed and there is no point pressuring me. Aaahhhhhhhhh! For now, the ball is in my court. You both need to behave. Leave! Start with fixing my windows,' I demanded loudly.

Thinking deeply, I gathered some courage and was noticing how each broken piece of glass was joined back to where it was. The window was intact and my room was spic and span.

'I am not your slave and maybe I do deserve a decent sleep alright. I shall continue watching Downton Abbey while you both disappear. Don't appear if you are not needed or I don't call you. Literally, I mean it.'

Sarah and Thomas uttered no word. Their faces showed a gloomy sensation and eyes depicted a ray of hope. They waved at me and simply vanished.

I remembered my chat with Edwin again. After all, I did not only speak to ghosts but was actually pressured to be on a mission for them.

Life was no humor, but had become an adventure with spirits. History was not only spoken about but felt. The pages to my future lied in the hands of supernatural power where I was nothing less than a marionette. For something to be fulfilled, one had to declare a war against all odds, I believed.

There was no escape plan. Even if this was like an act of despair there was no salvation. The suffocation had to be embraced with glee.

## CHAPTER 12

# The First Class with a Twist

Erasing words that were written a day before can be a form of exercise the next day. The ink does not seem to leave its mark. The students had drawn random stuff on the magnetic whiteboard that it was getting a little tough for me to wipe it off. Sigh! This is my first day of class for grade ten and this is not helping. Well I shall ignore this and continue with introducing myself, I thought.

As I turned around, I put down the pen, and took out my compass. I took a few steps forward and placed the compass on the desk placed on the third row.

I thought of a warmer to pep up the class and introduce myself in a creative way, but that became useless when I got busy cleaning the marks on the whiteboard and finding the attendance sheet. I found it on laying on the shelf as a student had asked where he could sit.

I went through the attendance sheet of twenty-five names quickly.

How silly of me or how annoying of Sarah to make me a fool in front of my new students! She kept the attendance sheet elsewhere. I did skip the warmer and continued with talking about Hawaii and the beaches. The students showed keen interest in knowing about the other side of the world.

One of the students, *Jude Gilliam*, seemed rather interesting. He seemed much more ignorant or innocent about the fun side of life.

When all the students had introduced themselves, even mentioning about what their parents did, Jude's dad's profession was rather uncommon. He worked as an undertaker for many years. I was surprised since I did hear that undertakers were not too respectful in the past to the deceased. Superstitions regarding death remain so strong that many people from various cultures avoided this kind of job and liked to stay away from dead bodies.

Jude's dad also started his funeral home and it had been running quite well for many years according to him. This whole thing about dead bodies and bereavement got me to think that I have simply entered a world where dead bodies and spirits are simply going to be my new chapter of life.

With a smirk, 'Jude, your dad's profession is quite an understatement and I am sure you have seen many dead bodies by now that Halloween doesn't seem scary but a fairy tale story.'

He laughed and with his contagious laughter the whole class was influenced with a moment of humor.

There was a sound of wind chimes in the class that everyone was looking around where it came from. The compass began to float up in the air circling in random directions. Everyone was simply stunned, but no one was scared surprisingly.

The room began to get cold. I did not expect it to be chilly. It was not a feeling of fear but the kind of emotion associated with the fact that death has united with the living in the classroom. I knew it. Sarah and Thomas had arrived.

The class had now begun with two unidentified studies and started with a twist. The compass then landed on the desk smoothly and everyone simply cracked up thinking that some lame magic had occurred.

Only Jude could sense that something was certainly strange about the situation, as I saw his eyes staring back at me asking me a million questions. He was biting his fingers, then rolling his pen, and closed his eyes for a few seconds. That clearly indicated something I did not know but probably he did know was yet to be found out eventually.

I told everyone to open to page twenty-one and start making some bullet points on the development of Sociology. They had fifteen minutes to skim through and it would then be carried on with a discussion.

I was ticking and separating some flash cards, and then I simply felt this shiver. To my surprise Thomas was standing beside Jude and reading what he wrote. My hands quivered, and I wanted to strangle Thomas for simply barging in the class like that. How could he? I couldn't believe this was happening . . . oh no.

I asked Jude to give me the compass so I could discuss the history and essential ways of using it with the class. Thomas slowly tilted his head and looked at me innocently.

He slowly had this wide smile only to remind me that he was here for his absolute date moment. He could not stop looking at the young girls around and he began to blow a current of air on one of the girls to feel the texture of her hair.

The fifteen year old was simply looking around wondering where the wind came from. She took her clip and twirled her hair up. Thomas tried blowing it again, but the clip would not move. He got annoyed that he realized he should not do anything further. He quietly left the room.

While the discussion went on, a feeling of relief was there that the first class was successful even with spirits around. The bell had rung and everyone got a lunch break.

I took my stuff and put it back in my leather bag.

Jude stayed back to accompany me out to the canteen. I was not as hungry so I told him he could carry on with his lunch. He refused politely and told me he would show me around the school.

He said with a slight sarcasm, "You must have seen the school, but you have not seen the real bit. There are some hidden getaways that I would like to show you. You seem different and on the cooler side."

'That was a quick judgment. Who knows I turn into a vampire and was waiting to sip your yummy blood. Well . . . thanks and I don't have much time to see many places that are not known to people but just one for now. Then I guess grabbing a quick bit would be a good idea, Jude,' I said jovially.

We walked about a kilometer away from the main school compound, then through the bushes. I saw this other waterfall place and continued walking pass that. Jude and I saw two boys crouched in shadows, injecting themselves with cocktails of synthetic drugs.

"Sorry, I did not bring you here to see this. We should hide behind the tree so we don't get caught looking at them," said Jude hurriedly.

'Ahh . . . okay! Who are these boys? Are they from our school? Oh yes, they are! I see the logo of HAVEN. Someone should stop them. This is crazy,' I said disappointingly.

"We can't!" Jude said with his eyes blinking.

It was the time where I could see his face clearly. He had high wide cheekbones that gave the impression of orange cheeks and his long lashes curled up like a fan.

His curled lashes were a distraction that I remembered, 'Yes, we can!'

"Not now. I remember, one day I followed this strange looking man going into a dark corner of a deteriorated building. There was cracked prescription bottles littered on the ground. He jabbed a syringe into his arm and injected the blend of drugs. And the other day, some school boys had visited some friends in this school . . ."

'How can they? This is not acceptable and it's bad. Wait, hold my books,' I said furiously.

I quickly took out my phone and quietly took out a video of the boy who looked like he was stoned and floating in another planet. After the recording, I slipped the phone back in my bag. Jude was gurgling with delight as if he was in a mission. I felt nature was looking down upon all of us disdainfully. I refused to go to any other secluded place and marched out of there breezily.

Jude could tell I was upset and he kept wondering what I would do. He tapped on my shoulder and I looked at him, 'How do you know about drugs? Like what was taken and what exactly happens?'

"Remember, my dad is an undertaker and I have seen many cases over the years," replied Jude sincerely.

I smiled, 'Well, can this be our secret and we should end this. So don't tell anyone anything. This can be a new silent project. For now it's better you focus on academics.'

We walked and then dispersed as if we became private detectives. I could not believe that I was interested in solving a new case with a student. It surely seemed like an adventure.

I paced toward the canteen and saw the clock. Gladly, I still had fifteen minutes. When I turned my shoulder, I bumped into Dominic.

Looking at his gray-blue eyes, slowly descending towards his hair that was slicked back stylishly, and his rich and sensual lips, manipulated my promise to not think of any man. His eyes seemed consumed with some profound emotion. I was influenced by his attractive appearance that slowly provoked me to have this slight pout depicting happiness.

I had nothing appropriate to say, so simply smiled bashfully and left to get a Turkey Caesar Salad Sandwich.

I didn't even want to look or know what he thought of me. I wanted to eat, teach and get back to my room. Now it was not about making a lesson plan for my class but another outline of how I would solve several problems. That was certainly not easy. Even though, Dominic looked attractive, I couldn't feel myself good enough to manage a relationship anymore. Managing emotional nonsense created by a relationship was hard work for me where I preferred to put the energy on something else.

Words failed to pass my lips; even if I tried I didn't want it to back fire. I was so done with this.

I had eaten and was ready for the grade twelve lesson, where an intensive class on gender inequality was to be described and discussed.

As I got up, took a can of Diet Coke and opened it. I was drinking it as if I had been separated it from ages. I know, fizzy drinks are like a big no, but all the unhealthy stuff is so not to be sacrificed when you need to balance your fluctuating mood.

I am in a foreign country with spirits and this attractive man is in front of me, but I got to play a sacrifice game. Yes, he is a tempting delight . . . Oh Lord; this is simply not funny.

I feel lost in the astral, angelic voices where I would want him to scoop me into his arms and kiss me.

How can one stay without passion, it was more like a human without a nervous system. Even a ghost would like to experience that tingly feeling. No wonder Thomas was bugging me about having a date. If I can feel like this alive, he is dead!

Phew! Sigh! Fine, breathe. Time to go!

I walked pass many corridors and still could not hide away from Dominic, this time he spoke.

"Why are you in a hurry?"

'Yup! Got to go,' I said hastily and continued pacing toward the classroom.

As usual, the class started off well. This time I switched on a song of *Black Eyed Peas – Where is the love* to break the ice for the topic. Really, where is the love? Gender issues don't stop. They have become better in some parts of the world but for some it never changed.

A good forty minute of discussion on the topic and the ten minutes of two short videos was an adequate lesson taught. I was refreshed and totally enjoyed it. The girls seemed to enjoy the class more than the boys when it came to prove or show off girl power with a debate.

After the video was shown, I had shut down the projector and was putting away some sheets into the folder.

I saw a small bullet next to the can of Diet Coke. I was marveled with the fact that a bullet was simply put there without even any supervision. But I couldn't totally tell what kind of bullet it was.

I took the bullet, put in the opening of the can, and threw it into the trash can.

I was given a small box of cookies by a group of girls who welcomed me and praised me for a fantastic class. I was thrilled and completely awed by the unexpected gesture. It was good to know that my first time as a teacher was not bad after all.

Thanking them with delight and seeing their joyful faces was a mission accomplished. I felt like setting up my own Glee club. Only thing was, I couldn't sing for nuts. Even birds would sing or chirp better.

After sometime, the class was empty. I sat there for some time and was pretty relaxed at that moment. I got up and was surveying the classroom. I went to the bookshelf and noticed many books with pictures of bullets and rifles on it. They did look intense and quite a pull to make one read about it.

When I took out one book from the shelf I saw the same bullet behind the book.

'Sarah and Thomas, this is not fun. Come out now and don't annoy me for heaven sake.'

It was no one and I waited for a while, but still no one appeared. Instead the number of bullets began multiplying that the whole room was filled with bullets.

As I rounded to the back corner of the class, I was confronted by a massive, dirt-encrusted figure that glowed with orange fire. The smell of rotting leaves and marsh grass filled my nostrils as I saw the bullets increasing. Then I heard a chuckle from behind the shelf but couldn't see anyone.

It was so hard to walk through or even step forward. I began slipping away and tripped over the bullets. It was painful, falling flat on my stomach and then noticing that the bullets were getting pulled toward the magnetic whiteboard forming a name of a person.

The name Viera was creatively written on the board. By then I tried to get the balance and noticed that I could stand in the middle and was completely covered with a circle of golden bullets.

I knew a supernatural force did have something to do with this again. But I was completely drained out to get caught up with a new sequence to a story. I called out the name Viera several times and finally the bullets were disappearing.

I wished I could vanish.

I hadn't known that I was going to be introduced to a new spirit. Only found out when I saw a shadow of a curly haired girl making her way through the bullets.

Pale and olive of skin, her brown eyes shined luminously, and her thin long arms wrapped themselves around the credulous, while tainted-green hands and spiky nails at the end of long bony fingers stroked me into the deepest fear.

She simply came and hugged me.

Oh, I was being embraced by a spirit. Her entry was scary. Her tainted-green hands—intense! Her ghostly tricks were not exaggerated.

"You have seen enough of tricks, so thought of making it mellow for you," said Viera with a soothing voice.

Swallowing my saliva, feeling terrified . . . seriously! Another spirit to accommodate now! This is hell!

I pushed away the girl and took a few steps backwards. As I did that I could see blood gushing out of her stomach.

She screamed, "I was struck by bullet on my knee, it deflected into my stomach, and boom."

I was feeling so dehydrated. What was happening? Who are these kids? A present for me from the 1960s, I thought curiously.

I missed my world of Barbie and eating every bite of Kiwi. Coming here is certainly a bad choice. Perhaps I got to speak to someone about this. I need help! I am not a pro in solving cases of dead people. I don't qualify for this shit.

I sat down on the chair with my hands on my head thinking if I could speak to Emily or Dominic about it.

No, I can't, like every movie, anyone who talks about ghosts they are judged and looked like a paranoid goof.

Fine! Wait a minute.

'Count to hundred Ashley!' I blurted out.

The little girl began to giggle at my random gestures and came right in front of me like she had slid quite fast.

I did not want to ask her about her death. The question was why has my first day of class started off with a twist leaving a bullet in my mind.

I need a cherry on my cake. All this is aggravating a pain that I had left behind. I could not feel stronger again, but rather it weakened me completely.

Tears were streaming down my cheeks. I couldn't stop myself from weeping like a baby.

I heard a knock on the door! I quickly wiped my tears, but how could I hide my red nose that would show something had happened.

I stood up, took the rest of the papers and put it in the file. The book had slammed down on the floor because of a surprise visit so I had to place it back on the shelf.

As I turned, he was there. I wanted to hide from another surprise visit.

## CHAPTER 13

# A Bullet a Day Keeps a Passion Away

It was definitely a surprise. What was Dominic doing here with Jude behind him? Dominic looked as sexy shaved and could I even tell him I have been welcomed by three crazy teen ghosts?

'Hey! What you guys doing here? Jude, is everything okay? Don't see a point of you doing anything here.'

"Why are you being so grouchy?" said Dominic his tone rasping.

'No, you sound insensitive. I am curious now, Dominic. Why are you picking an argument?'

Jude was silent and did not dare say a word knowing that he would be simply adding more stress to this sticky conversation for no reason.

Dominic sidled up next to me and slung his arm around my shoulders.

'Oh-ho! What was that?'

He whispered, "Stay away from the druggies. You are new here and there is no need to behave like some superwoman." Backing off slowly, I could see his seductive eyes and incandescent smile.

For a moment I forgot Jude was there. He stood there watching every move as if he was about to dissect the situation.

The fidgety movement of my fingers intertwined that showed I was getting nervous.

'There was no need to whisper. I don't know what you are talking about . . .'

"Yes, you do. Jude mentioned about your little trip to a secret getaway and your spy like nature that got you to take a video."

'Hey, Jude! You were the one who told me about that place and now I am a spy. What's going on? Come here right now!'

"Ms. Ashley, you don't have to be upset. I thought it would be better if Mr. Dominic know about the situation since he has been there before and knows a lot about it."

'Uff . . . you know what . . . you guys just leave. Phew, I have no interest or any sort of inclination to dabble between situations and intervene between both of your secret plans. You are right . . . I am new here.'

"Am sorry Ms. Ashley, it was not to offend you nor create any sort of judgment. I have a next class. See you later." Jude, left the room leaving me with a man whom I thought was charming and now I could even kill him. Damn, he is annoying.

Carrying my folder from the table and the fleeting thought reminded me about Viera. And now Dominic was right there observing my gestures. Why doesn't he leave?

Biting my lower lip and the deep feeling to literally scream was igniting like an active volcano. As I paced a few steps ahead passing him without any eye contact, "Ashley," he said in a soothing voice.

'What now. I don't need to be interrogated here. Thanks for the warning in a seductive way. You didn't have to be so dramatic. I have better things to do. You can be happy with your new adventure . . . umm . . .'

"You thought I was being seductive?" Dominic asked intriguingly. His grin, however, stroked my nerves into an overheated state of awareness.

'Oops.'

"Oops . . . Ashley! Really!"

I couldn't look into his eyes and with a brisk movement I left the room. Oh no . . . now he must be thinking I am really a lunatic. Or he probably thinks I am some sort of a sleazy person. Well, I don't care, he did point out his warning not in a right form of gesture. Who cares, I am glad I am out of there. I need space now.

Everyone is crazy here. And I guess I am getting in that crazy zone sooner or later. What was bothering me more was Viera. What new twist was this now?

Sitting in the staff room, surveying the ceramic vases, and then writing short notes on my brown antique looking diary about Sarah, Thomas and Viera was infuriating. I wanted to speak to Dominic about it, but now that shall be evaporated like a bad dream. Reading through the short notes on what happened to these children got me flustering between thoughts.

Placing the pen down and taking a sip of the warm cappuccino was soothing. The blend of espresso and milk in a light fluffy texture awakened the senses of a weary soul.

To my surprise the pen was slowly floating in the air. The cup of cappuccino fell of my hand and bang on the floor. I stood up in dismay. No one was in the staff room, so definitely no witness.

The pen took its suitable position by rolling around in circular movements until the tip of it began penning down something on my diary. I was shocked!

I quickly went to get some tissue and began clearing the broken cup and threw it in the bin. Looking upward from a distance I see a flow of words written but as a poem.

The birth of new creeks was definitely looming from a threatening horizon as I begun reading . . .

Burying away youth,
Abducted by swarthy Pirates,
Molesting the age of innocence,
Amulet of love surrendered,
The cry of losing ties ripped away.

No dolls, No laughter, No food,
Flames of disgust weeping away,
Dripping blood, greedy mind,
Appetite filled with bullets,
Yearning for salvation.

Someone bring care,
Someone bring justice,
Someone bring pain-killers,
You are the chosen one,
You bring light.
Yours...V

The entire poem spoke the unspoken. Viera was killed by pirates. The thought of it got me feeling nauseated. The poison of justice by these ghosts was poking every nerve of mine that to escape the scenario was inevitable.

With a harsh cry, my diary flew through the open windows of the staff room and vanished into a storm.

With an effort I managed to get out of the windowpane. Jumping down on the grassland was not painful. The temperate climate was hit by the unpredictability of a ghostly power where a preview of another dark story was to be shared.

The sweat under my arms and trembling feet was shadowed by a gloomy weather. The sky was overcast with thick clouds. There had been a great deal of rain, and now the wind was very high and blew the dry leaves across the road in a shower. The words were scarcely out of my mouth when there was a growl, a splitting sound, and tearing, colliding down among the other trees ragged up by the roots, and it fell right across the road just before me.

I was pulled into the storm and the twisting force of nature handicapped every move. The fragrance of the mushy soil and salty water empowered my sensation to visualize an old pirate ship with swarthy pirates.

The weak voice penetrated into a shriek that pierced through my stomach. The peculiar smell of blood had drowned me into a well of repugnance. The wind seemed to have lulled off after that furious blast which tore up the tree. It grew darker and darker, calmer and calmer.

I could see a pale-skinned young teenage girl from a distance with curly blond hair and presumed it was Viera. She howled in agony and flapped away to a private corner to bleed in misery slowly closing her eyes. She could fly like a bird gracefully and slowly descended into my arms like a baby.

Her keen eyes were searching for relief and her tears of blood seeking justice. For a few seconds I looked at her intently that felt time had frozen.

"My name is *Viera Katz*, a fourteen year old Israeli."

The words out of her mouth shook me that I abandoned her. I paced backwards and saw myself floating in the air.

"Ashley, I began a perilous journey away from the pirates seeking to bring light to my dark world. You can help me! I am straddling between two worlds. Please say, YES!"

'Say Yes for what! This is terrible, frightening, and sucking out energy out of my system. My stomach hurts like crazy. The bullets are piercing through my organs. Please stop this feeling, Viera. I plead.'

The heat emitted from the bodies was intense. The piercing feeling was subsided. Slowly feeling my feet on the grassland brought a comforting feeling. It was the sound of laughter and children's voice that got my attention. I looked around and noticed I was alone and the collision of voices was from afar.

The faint feeling was battling my stamina to cope with all these ghostly tricks. Blood, death, revenge, and I were ingredients' to a new dark story.

'How many of you are there? I am so sick of this. Have mercy to my tired bones. I have seen enough and now I cannot do this anymore. Please!'

Viera stood diagonal to me and watched me anguish. The storm was over. But Sarah and Thomas appeared standing next to Viera.

The three thirsty vengeances were glaring into my eyes as if I was to be hypnotized and develop a new outline to my life.

'How many of you are there? I want to know it now! Now! Now!'

There were two children scampering about, to the distraction of their parents. An older boy and a ruffled haired little toddler had distracted the tensed moment. I waited for them to pass by and turned around.

My skin crawled and I glanced down at my hand, noting that my hair was standing on one end. I was shocked and everything seemed blurry that my skin was deathly pale and I was about to faint.

Thump!

## CHAPTER 14

# The Unwanted Persuasion

My vision was fuzzy, and my head was floating. Everything went pitch black as darkness took over me. When I woke up, I felt a little twinge in the back of my head. I was astounded as if I was just given a shock therapy.

There were three more ghosts standing in front of me as I lay on the grass. The six spirits had surrounded me as if was to be gulped by them.

I was tormented by an act of an unwanted persuasion. My eyes squinting to a ray of light to identify the other three spirits was an effort.

"You look terrible! These are my friends: *Edward Foreman* and *Judy Lee,*" said Thomas with a wink.

'You have friends in ghostland? Aaahhhhhh! Who is that one?'

"Oh, he is *Roy Demir,* my friend," said Viera with her soft voice.

Very gently I get the balance to stand as Sarah offers her hand. 'Now you guys are six ghosts! What am I to you guys? Everything is so freaky. Now what should I have a tea party for all of you so you can introduce yourself. I am going nuts! I cannot take this anymore . . .'

Leaving the six spirits to seek the pleasure of their timepass, I paced toward the staffroom. I noticed my diary on the grass, so picked it up and sauntered away.

Sitting back on my leathered chair, I wept away like a baby. Something has surely gotten into me I contemplate. Some things are meant to be out of reach then how can the ghosts come to being associated with people alive. Dead should be dead.

The sound of the ripping of papers came from behind and I kept silent instantly. I hope no one heard me.

As I turn around, Dominic was staring at me with concern. He was quiet for some time until he stood up and started to walk towards me.

The momentarily situation was not an amusement. I have nothing to say to him and he cannot know about the ghosts. He already thinks I am barbaric and I should take my stuff and leave back to my apartment.

Looking back at my papers on the table, I briskly take each paper and put it into a folder. Placing my Mac back into the case, there was a tap on my shoulder. Sigh!

'Please leave me alone. I have loads to do and this is not a good time for a friendly chat.'

"I know it's not the time for a friendly chat, but the time to clarify what you said earlier about me seducing you. That was certainly not my intention, however, something must be bothering you that you blurted such an accusation," said Dominic calmly.

'I did not accuse you of anything, it was just your body language and I blurted. Look I really got to go.'

Being more pragmatic than I, he just smiled at me, "Okay, as you please." He moved back a few steps and I took a few steps forward passing him.

Having paused, 'It was nothing Dominic, so don't think of anything else.'

"Hmm . . . why were you crying?"

'You saw that?'

"I heard that."

'I thought I was in my quiet zone, did not know I had company.'

"You might always have company. This is the staff room, Ashley."

I couldn't say anything and walked away. Dominic was stunned with the abrupt behavior and from his voice he surely did seem he wanted to dig in for more information.

It was more like I had some much to say and someone had chopped my imaginary tongue. The procrastination of fate to solve the trauma was nibbling every bit of hope. The overwhelming weight of fear and darkness pushed the essence of confidence into a tunnel of doubt.

Walking through the corridor I hear a group of students singing for their drama class. I watch them from a distance feeling elated. Their world away from supernatural awareness was what I really longed for.

Mannequins of cowboys lounged around with playing cards, and the drama teacher took a place behind the polished bar and conversed the role of the bar in the days of the gold rush. I was absolutely fascinated. I was listening with half an ear as I poked around the room and observed the exhibits, trying to imagine what it was like to drink and play cards underground, having gold in my pocket and a gun at my side. The feeling was kind of cool. The students were rehearsing for their play.

Trying to balance the weight of laptop case, my folders, and the burden of six ghosts were suppressing me as if I was about to be pushed underground. And that's when I was hit with the first wave of wobbliness. I swayed as my eyes swam with strange, out-of-focus colors. My stomach flip-flopped oddly, my spine went stiff, and the skin on my shoulders and arms prickled with goose bumps. For a moment, I could hear sounds of water swishing and a girl's voice right by my ear said something in Asian. I gasped and whirled, but no one was there.

It was either Japanese or Korean I figured, but who could distinguish it since it had been a while I heard the language. The feeling of staying there longer was a bad idea as if the ghosts were always parading wherever I went.

Alarmed by my experience, I tried to stay close where there were people before something else happened.

Feeling anxious and scared, I finally did reach my room without a new supernatural act. I blinked vigilantly as I looked around the room, but everything stayed in focus, for which I was thankful.

I couldn't tell what would keep me calm or even for a moment those incidents erased from my memory would have been a boon.

Half a load was placed on the kitchen table, but what could one do with an intangible weight of chaos. I was so exhausted that I didn't even realize when my head rested on the table.

The vicious croaking sound of frogs and the slithering sound of snakes woke me up with a shock. 'I am going to die today!'

I looked at the clock and noticed I slept for two hours. 'Oh my, I must have been in coma. What happened to me?'

The ambience of the room depicted my gloomy mood. It had to be cheered up so I could get some work done. Having lit rose tea candles, I then switched on the table lamp and walked to switch on instrumental piano music.

The harmonious sound crawled into my system with a comfortable fluidity. Within a few seconds my nervous system was relaxed. My thought process was back to normalcy. Now it was easy to comprehend the whole scenario with the ghosts and Dominic.

Sitting on the sofa and having a sip of peach lemon tea quenched the deprived stomach from any authentic flavor. It seemed that the mind had signaled for a boost and emphasized on a focus approach to the whole bizarre confrontations.

I gathered all the papers and circled what had to be done for the next class. Then the next episode of Downton Abbey was being watched without any intervention which came to a surprise, how grateful I was.

Having thought of this, I was interrupted by Thomas's croaky sound. A sudden shudder dives into my spine getting me back to focus. They would not even leave me alone.

'What is it Thomas?'

"How was your sleep? And you seem better now. I can see you have settled in a comfort zone . . ."

'Stop it! Everything you say is not funny. Who are you here with? I am sure you would bring your friends from ghostland.'

"You are getting good at this. Yes, Judy and Edward are here."

'So what is it now? What new dark story. I should not be teaching now, its better I started writing tales of the dead,' I snapped a little sharply.

The sound of the gong being hit repeatedly started to get louder. The flame of the candle rose and flickered dancing to the tunes of sound of the gong. Slowly making her appearance, Judy came to a physical appearance. I could see her with her short black her. She looked adorable with her hazel eyes. The innocence of her adolescence was shadowed by her mysterious story.

I took a deep breath and another until my irritation began to ware. Thomas's smile grew mischievous, one corner of his mouth rising higher than the other. It was better to ignore his face and look at Judy.

"This evening it was me who you heard at the drama rehearsal," Judy confided.

"Feisty little snip, isn't she?" said Edward muttered.

'Oh Lord! When did you arrive?'

Edward gazed around the room, silently appraising Ashley's interior that accommodated her work space, while Judy eyed Edward speculatively.

I could smell Edward's minty and muddy fragrance. His hands rested on his knees as if he was ready to share his story.

Judy sat quietly taking a glance of my belongings. I wondered how old she would be.

Clearing his throat, "I guess you should hear Edward's story," distracted Thomas from my inquisitive thoughts.

'Oh you are a conniving little fool!'

The three ghostly figures were seated around me with their relaxed position and their eyes penetrated an expression to be heard.

It seemed they had eyes only for me, and courted me with a passion and zeal that swiftly had to win my heart to lend my ears to the tales of dark lands.

This was an unwanted persuasion to rekindle my spirits to express my compassion to the dead, where there was no other way.

The only way was one way and to be driven to another flashback of agony.

## CHAPTER 15

# Dungy Poaching

Edward was shaking his legs while Thomas lay down on my bed. Their gestures were getting me anxious and curious about Edward's story. The sleep in my eyes vanished when Sarah made her grand entrance from the toilet.

It kept me wondering how she came from there. Even though I wanted to ask her I thought it was better not to get there and listen to the next episode of flashback.

Sarah sat on top of the bookshelf. Her eyes turned green. It had a dark-blue rim around the iris and a lot of gold-orange around the pupil. With that slowly the bookshelf changed to the color of her eyes. The mystery behind the camouflage was speechless. It came to a point whether I was to be too scared or it was becoming an adaptation to a new trick.

There was a moment of silence. Edward bounded energetically into the center of the room, "Come to me, foul spirits!" he intoned loudly.

Judy unlocked the front door, and it opened with an ominous creak. I swallowed nervously and armpits sweating. I could feel like I was one of them. Disgusting!

Then I saw a ray of white light as if I was in a movie theatre and the projector was on. There was a countdown from five to one and I could then view the jungle. There were a group of people poaching for animals. There was blood everywhere.

Everything seemed so real. It was sad to see elephants killed and amount of ivory seized for illegal trade. Some included valuable parts of the animals' bodies. Even though there were different drives that caused poachers to perform the excruciating acts, it was simply intolerable to proceed with these evil acts through violence of some sort. I only read them in papers and had never seen anything live as such.

I wanted to throw up as I saw what the poachers did. To remove the tooth of the elephant it was carved out of the skull. The poachers shot the elephant and started to cut it into pieces. There was splash of blood everywhere. It was insane to see how each adult elephant tusk was embedded within the skull of the animal. It seemed to be five to six feet long. It was huge. This was no geography channel; it was a live beastly act.

It appeared that the poachers were on a killing spree when the next scene moved to hunting for the rhino horn. Being aware internally that rhino's horn is often grounded into powder and used to make traditional medicine, and watching the entire process was gross.

The rhino was shot dead and then a dagger was pierced into it. The horn was simply chopped off as if it was trash and the rhino was left there. It was disgusting!

Then there were sounds of gun shots. It became louder until I saw the wildlife officials chasing after a group of men where a Korean and Black man were shot continuously. There were sounds of women and children screaming and running out of their tents from a distance until there was a pin drop silence.

There was a field of dead women and children. I recognized Edward and Judy. They were shot brutally because of the act of their fathers. They paid the price for the greedy trade and in a moment their childhood was buried because of the cold and materialistic pleasures.

The projection came to an end. The front door of the room was shut with a loud bang. I felt feverish and did not know where to start. The sound of someone sniffing got my attention where I saw Judy wiping her tears.

The poor little thing was crying like a baby and Edward was pretending to be fearless. I could feel like I gained consciousness but the bottom line was what I was supposed to do to help them set free. The puzzle was definitely hard to solve. I did not know where to start.

Scratching his head, "Because of manipulation, gluttony, and indifference our lives were gone. There were never harsh penalties to protect neither the animals nor the children. We did not know much about poaching as our fathers told us to help the mothers in agriculture. They wanted to be rich and travel to Korea . . ." said Edward with frustration.

"And . . . umm . . . Edward's and my dad were good friends. They always talked about getting rich and doing all sorts of things illegally. I always overheard them until one day, Edward's father threatened me that if I ever told anyone he would chop my nose of like the rhino's," expressed Judy with worry.

Panic twinged inside me as I felt my feet trembling when I stood up to pace toward Judy. 'I won't have you all tarnish my reputation with all these shady stories. Just tell me what to do? Please leave me alone!'

Tears were flowing as I dropped to the ground pleading to be set free. 'I am sorry all that happened to you. I cannot help you.'

There was a tap on my shoulder and hands embracing my waist for me to stand up slowly. When I titled my head to see who it was Sarah had embraced me while Thomas was holding my shoulders. They helped me stand up and I slumped down back on the sofa.

I couldn't sit. I needed fresh air, so I peeked through the windows on the first floor. I saw Zuri snoozing peacefully in a bunk bed. He looked warm and content away from all the ghostly mystification.

My swollen eyes looked back at the five ghosts. I wondered what the last spirit had left to say. How would Roy's story be any different?

My tired brain could not sustain the agony of death and vengeance. It yearned for a clean and crisp fresh breath of air.

It seemed that the character in my life spoke in a somber voice. I was forced to play a role I never envisioned I was even entitled to. I could smell a scent of cigar smoke then the smell turned to the burning of leaves. The strong odor got me coughing and I saw the five young spirits slowly being covered by fog. I couldn't see anything.

The room was cloudy and the strong odor of smoldering leaves began to be sucked out through the key hole where in a moment the room was empty—Crystal clear. Who could tell that there was a visit by spirits who had dark tales but didn't look scary or evil! But they were.

There was a knock on my door. It was getting enough and I needed to be left alone with my desolation without being harassed over and over again. As I walked to open the door, "Hey!" said Dominic with a bottle of wine.

'Seriously!'

"Why not Ashley! You were in a terrible shape earlier so thought a glass of wine would ease out your frustration of seduction," said Dominic with a tease.

'I don't need this right now.'

"Oh well, should I come back later for another round to seduce you?" winked Dominic.

'You're not gonna leave right. What if I said, there's a ghost behind you. Would you leave?'

"I am not buying that. There's nothing. I see you! You're the living ghost and come on, don't be a lunatic."

'B-b-b-u-t there are five ghosts. I saw them, D . . .'

"You sound like a nervous wreck and that was not a good way to chase me out. I am coming in," entered Dominic and walked toward the pantry.

He took out two coffee cups and poured the open bottle of red wine into them.

"It's good I had opened the bottle before I came here . . ."

'What if I wasn't in the room?'

"You were so there is no if and no but. Here take the cup and take a deep breath, I am not here to seduce you. I am engaged and its a few months now. You're not my type—you're a lunatic who spies druggies and sees ghosts," said Dominic with a laugh.

'Hmm . . . thanks for coffee . . . umm . . . wine. We can sit on the sofa. Seriously, why are you here?'

"Just . . . getting bored and needed a company of red wine in a coffee cup," Dominic said in a low tone.

Smiling, 'Well, thanks, wine in a coffee cup is good. I guess this is what I needed. Don't you miss your fiancé?'

"I do—work is work. We are busy with our career and catch up on and off. How about yours married—kids?"

'Nah—was engaged and now back to embrace my ambition. There has been a big change from being an archeologist to a teacher now. The students do get me on my toes.'

"Sure, they do. Tomorrow there is a luncheon at school for all the teachers. There was an announcement when you were not there, so thought of informing you. Like last year, Miss Orchestra will bring her peach and blueberry cobbler. Everyone raves about it. It's delightfully sinful. It's like after everyone eats it, everyone feels different. You should come and take a bite. That crunch into relishing dessert would surely seduce you."

'Not funny Dominic. Did it bewitch you? Were you charmed by the peaches?'

"You do have a sense of humor. So bring that tomorrow, Ashley."

'Okay Mr. Sarcastic. And thanks for the wine, again.'

Dominic got up and paced towards the door, "Sleep tight!" he said picturing the flash of sleep in my eyes.

'You're a master piece. How does your fiancé put up with your cheeky humor? Good night and see you tomorrow,' I said pushing Dominic slowly out of the room.

After closing the door, a sense of easement was crawling down every vein. Dominic did bring a smile on my face. His wit got me to loath him as much for having such an effect on me.

'Oh well—he is engaged! Ping!'

Keeping the cups in the sink, switching off the lights, and making sure the door and windows all locked took me back to my serene sanctuary.

## CHAPTER 16

# The Luncheon

Here I was all prepared for the lunch, Dominic had raved about and he was not even here. Observing the dining room with its mix of rich red and peachy wallpaper reminded me of a night when Edwin had proposed to marry me at this bar in Hawaii named 'Exquisite.' The few seconds of a snail flashback got me back to reality realizing I was back to being single again. We had already broken up and that's why this whole new teaching career came into picture. And zap—I was captivated with the interior of the dining room.

The décor had 19$^{th}$ century silks and matching furniture. The furniture was made up of fine hardwoods such as rosewood or mahogany, inlaid with carved designs, as I was touching the smooth flow of carving. The art deco antiques were Victorian and also from America that was made up of various materials from iron to zebra skin. They attributed the bold use of swaying curves, chevron patterns and sunburst ornamentation.

Everything nowadays was contemporary and chic whereas this school, 'HAVEN' sustained an era of elegance and class of its own.

There was this big French designed mirror which resembled the start of a cleavage of a beautiful woman's breasts. The oval shaped mirror was embedded with sparkling crystals leaving a curious question about its history when I saw the name—Roy carved on it. I was wondering which Roy this could be.

D-a-m-n! Now this would be interesting. What if the mirror had something to do with the spirit, Roy? Before I got crazier I looked away and had to find out. My skin felt weird as the smoothness was manipulated by the tingling fear of some sort.

Taking a few steps ahead, I see a cone shaped mudbrick decor. I had never seen a 3D shaped mudbrick of about four feet tall. It was intriguing and I wanted to know what was inside. Was there even anything? Inquisitive me!

Touching the texture of this cone shaped decor, I could feel dents of clay in it. The model depicted African architecture as it had African art painted on it. Various shapes of pottery and types of masks were carved on the model. There were a few key holder hooks inside it and one was slightly longer than the rest, so I touched it and the hook twisted facing the opposite direction. The model opened and I quickly unfastened the mud wall leading me into several masks, impressive gold sculptured elements, and a heart shaped clay box.

It was gorgeous. The hidden piece of décor inside the cone shaped decor was surely kept discreetly to save it from being stolen, I presumed.

'Oops!' This better shut before someone accuses me of stealing anything. Some teachers were around and chuckling at my lumbering behavior.

Everything seemed quite costly and worth every historical tale. The entire model was sophisticated and created oomph of African heritage kept in the open in the dining room. Each show piece was worth every peek.

As I looked further, I saw the next section of the dining room; a corrugated iron roof was above the concrete ceiling, which was obviously built as it would heat up in the sun, drawing air from inside the library up through the clay pot holes to cool the dining room. The center of this section of the dining room was lit with dappled light. A rectangular area around the room was enclosed by a portico of columns made of eucalyptus. The vague minty fragrance was soothing. The merge of African and English architecture was fascinating.

There was no one in this side of the dining room. Everyone seemed to crowd the first section and were pretty much engrossed with gossips and various cuisines.

From a distance ahead I could see a stone staircase. Since no one was around, the curious mind was thinking of mischievous acts. Without being appalling, I walked ahead and went up the stairs.

A glass wall was built between the living areas and the terrace folds completely away to generate one huge living space, with the second lounge area leading onto the backyard where a master bedroom, dressing room and a light-filled en-suite views over the pool outside. The dining area below was the opposite of the second floor.

Why was there a master bedroom and a pool up here? Perhaps it was where Principal Orchestra resided. She surely got an elite treatment. That was distinguished clearly.

Hearing to the loud chatters of teachers I came down the stairs and saw Dominic speaking to Elma for a distance. They couldn't see me.

As I walked pass the second section of the dining room, Elma waved and called me to join her.

"Were you there? I saw you walking. Did you snoop around?" asked Elma with a wink.

'Yes, I did.'

"So you actually got to see the special guest house up there," stated Elma curiously.

'You know that?'

"No, I heard about it," spoke Elma anxiously.

'That's a guest house! I thought it was where Orchestra stayed.'

"Well . . . she has a better place. Her stay is at a courtyard behind this place," interrupted Dominic.

"Yup Ashley, she has two rooms, the antique library, types of swords hanging on the walls and some masks if I remember. I got to see it for a few minutes last year because of some paperwork," added Elma.

"So what's in the next dining room, Ashley," asked Dominic.

"Do you know that other dining room ahead is made entirely of mudbrick and lamps around?" expressed Ashley.

'Oh okay. It was a cozy and a well made dining area. But no one was there. It looks as if it's being preserved for its décor,' said Ashley looking at Elma.

'I love different architecture . . .' added Ashley.

"And you also love ghosts," teased Dominic.

'Not funny . . . D . . .'

The sound of a clinking glass bell caught everyone's attention.

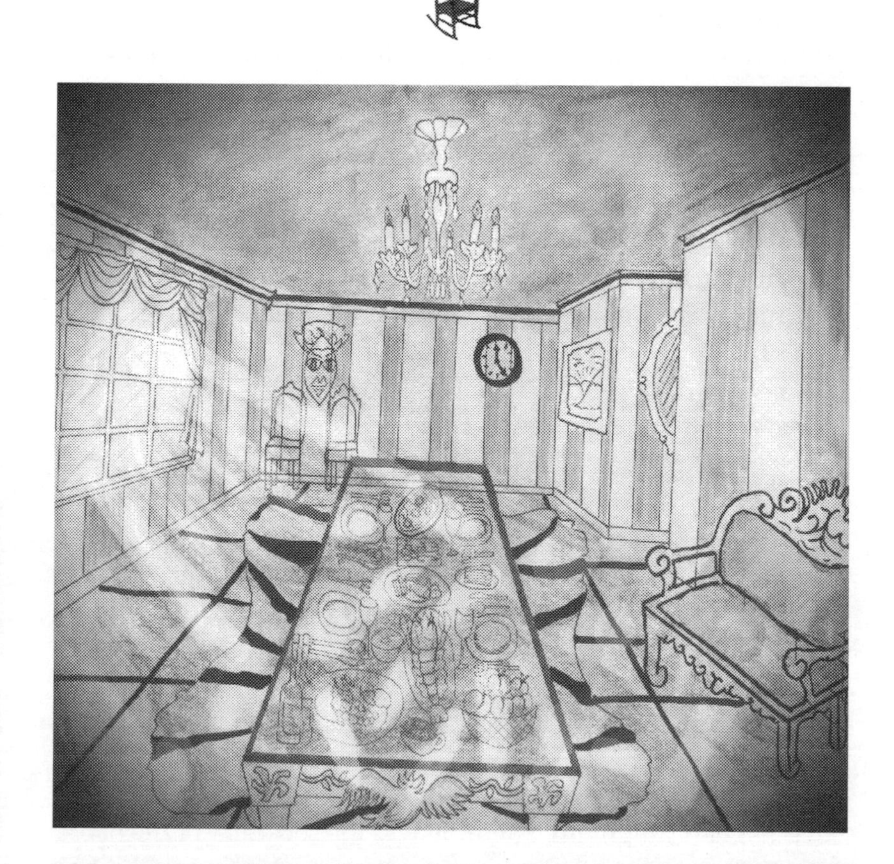

Dominic held my hand and escorted me in front to see the scrumptious cuisine. The marble table was decorated with various cuisines. I spotted—peach and blueberry cobbler. When taking a glance at Dominic, he was already observing my reaction seeing the luncheon. His eyes teased my motions as he was slowly getting closer to me.

This man was certainly up to something again. He couldn't stop flirting and he was engaged for goodness sake. I stepped back and grabbed myself a plate. The awkward feeling because of him made me feel giddy.

Placing two small chunks of devil food cake, a piece of the peach and blueberry cobbler, a spoon of mash potato, a slice of ham, and the Greek salad for the first serving was enticing. The food certainly looked tempting and the luncheon sent a sweet sentiment of an imaginary holiday.

"You eat pretty little, dig in. And—are you alright," said Dominic apprehensively.

'I am. Now shall we savor the cuisine?'

From Dominic's reaction, I could sense that he could tell my voice threatened to crack as my gestures were slightly clumsy.

After a welcome speech, Principal Orchestra offered me a glass of wine smiling politely welcoming me to the school. Her gesture comforted my feelings temporarily away from the dark tales and calmed my nervous system. But she seemed different today. I couldn't tell what exactly it was, except that she was enveloped with sweet words.

Principal Orchestra left to get some food whilst Dominic was gobbling his food. How silly he looked. His carefree attitude did have some charm. As he was slurping the spaghetti, he winked at me just like a teenager. Oh this man will never learn or change, I thought.

The luncheon was no less than a feast and the treat the teachers received was a commendable bribe to contemplate once again to stay longer at the school.

What had caught my attention was the scripture of the name Roy on the mirror. Why was it even there and who could it be?

Or perhaps it was some kind of a playful act and now it must have disappeared.

Striding towards the mirror, the stylish signature was still there and as I looked up I saw a reflection on the mirror.

I turned behind and saw no one. The game of another dark tale had begun as if someone had granted a momentary pleasure with an obligation.

Looking back at the mirror, I could see deep-set eyes. His eyes were big and resembled the eyes of a frog. It was terrifying to see the color change from dark gray to golden. My hands began to tremble; standing there longer was a terrible idea.

I have to l-e-a-v-e. Oh NO! Why is my nose bleeding? I have to LEAVE.

# CHAPTER 17

# Blood Feud

Blood was dripping. There was no way of stopping it. And no one could see it. I was draped in a blood pool.

I just could not describe the look of disbelief and horror. Suddenly, with an immense roar, a tractor materializes from nowhere and at that exact moment the headlights flicked on catching my attention.

It was Zuri. He was going somewhere and offered me a ride towards the exit where the apartment was. This was a blessing in disguise.

"Bye Ashley. You seem put off. Get some rest." Zuri drove away and my head was spinning. Getting back into my room was like my goal now.

All these spirits were preaching hate and violence was portrayed stabbing my sane personality. I became a victim of their unfortunate fate.

Unlocking the door, I grabbed ice from the freezer and rubbed it on my nose.

'Aaaah—this stings.'

"Yes—it does," a husky voice is being echoed in my room. Surveying my room quickly, I see no one. The lethargic body gave up on me. My eyes took control as it decided to embrace a moment of solitude.

Moments later, as I opened my eyes, I realized that my nose was not bleeding anymore and I was lying on my sofa. I couldn't remember when did I even come this far.

Clearing his throat, "Don't be confused and take the stress, I brought you here," said Roy.

'What on earth are you even doing here? Who gave you the permission to invade my minuscule pleasure of time? Can't any of you even feel the grief?'

Roy was sitting on the bed wearing a cotton white T-shirt with red denim shorts.

"We do! That is w-h-y, we are here," said Roy cheekily.

'You are very corrupt, writhing, full of crap, little monster.'

"There were far too many descriptions. Make up your mind what exactly am I, Ashley. You have heard everyone's story, now it's my turn. You can't be so cruel can you . . ."

'Shut up Roy!'

"Calm down Ashley"

'Just shut up Roy!'

"This case is not closed Ash-ley. I have come a long quest for justice from a blood feud and this has to be heard."

'It is not like I was born with a talent of seeing ghosts or was I. I don't even understand this whole thing. How I can even cater to dead people after so many years. I never—never—never had this experience. Shucks!'

"Listen to me. For a second, mute your voice and take this as a gift and you would never hear us again. A flock of cells has been fostering over the years and a ray of hope was seen through you. There has never been an occasion that I have celebrated without despair. Stop being difficult and listen. Or else!"

'This is no joke! You cannot manipulate me and take charge of my life. For a second only I shall mute and a whole moment of displeasure will be dived in. I cannot even harp for peace. Roy, I know I have no CHOICE. So—SHOOT!'

His eyes were dark blue and it was seeking for peace. He slowly came out of his troubled mind and began to contemplate his urgency of narrating his story.

'You are tall! How old are you?'

"Aha—I am fifteen years old. Let's get on shall we. My mother never let me go to school or play with other children. She was always worried I would be gunned down the street. Umm . . . long before I was born, my father had killed a friend in a drunken state that sparkled a series of retaliatory killings after that. There was always vengeance for murder by killing family members just to prove power. Have you heard of Blood Feud?"

'Yes—oh—were you . . .'

"Aha—I was—GUNNED DOWN! It is the most absurd behavior in our civilization. This has been carried on for generations and many families have to live in isolation for years. I have been one of them. Living in isolation and seeing everything bleak has been a punishment. Until one day, I geared up some confidence and took fresh air. THAT WAS IT—BOOM! I was killed in that very room which is today a dining room for a luncheon. That mirror belonged to our family. It was the only thing left from my home. I WANT THAT MIRROR BACK!"

'Hell no! So it is your name that was carved on it. I was wondering which Roy it would be. And how would we get the mirror back. Oh Roy, this is all getting so messy and very hard on me. Now the new story is MIRROR. Oh no . . . is there blood all over my bed?'

"Your Principal stole the mirror! And there is no—NO for an answer."

'That was very demanding you BLOODY Roy! Oh my head—ufffff . . .'

"Check behind the mirror. You will get the answer. Now you heal from your unstable mind and see you soon at the dining table," said Roy archly.

He vanished and the blood stained bed was completely clear as if not even a drop was there. The numbness in my throat and nose was unbearable leaving cold shivers up my spine. I walked into the bathroom to unbutton my blood stained shirt.

To my surprise—there was nothing—ABSOLUTELY NOTHING!

'AAAaaaaaaaaaah! These ghosts have left me like peasants—so poor that without their charity—I can't even smile or breathe.'

Why would Principal Orchestra steal the mirror? What could possibly be written behind the mirror? All these mysteries would surely get me more paranoid.

I better draft an idea map about the next mission—WISH LIST OF THE SPIRITS! That could help me understand what they need before each of them savor every drop of blood I have in my body.

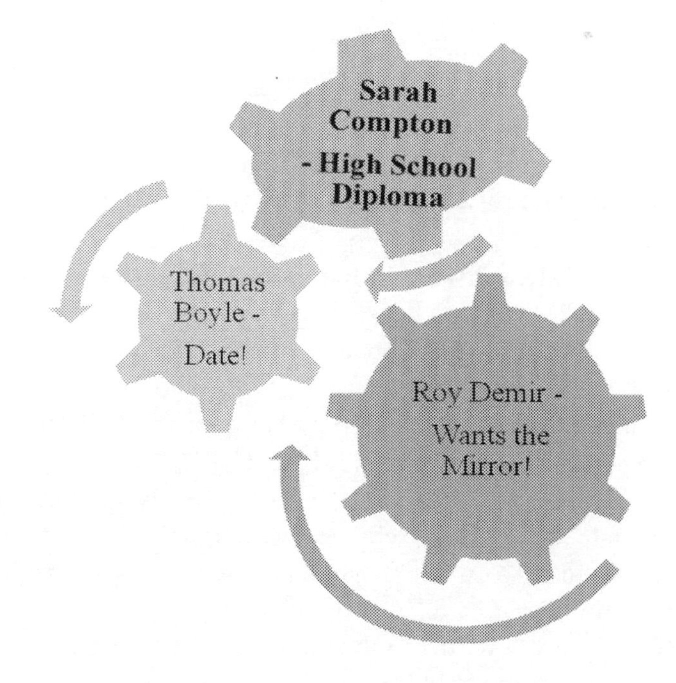

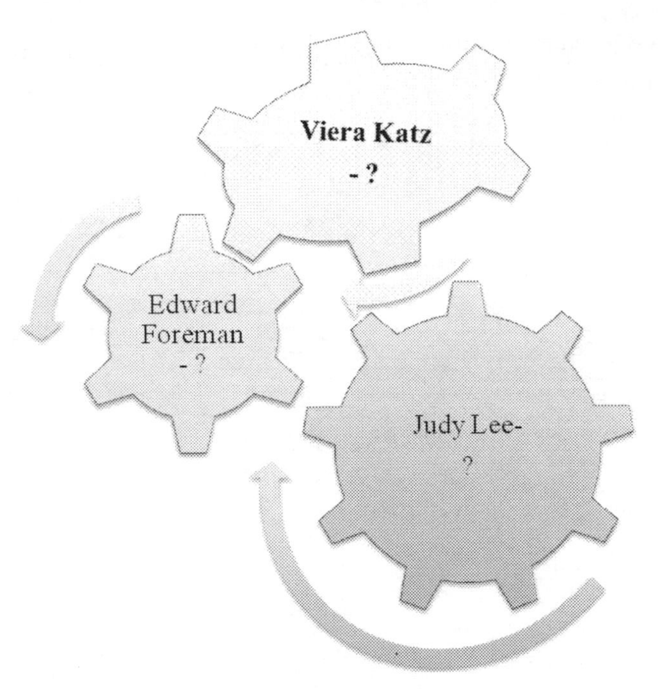


Hmm . . . I know what Sarah, Thomas, and Roy wants—how about Viera, Edward, and Judy! Now that seems like a big problem!

Viera and Edward were in the room and I knew they could see me as terror struck my heart. They could feel every sensation I was going through. They left that moment for the next day, I supposed.

"Ashley seems to feel cheated by her own spark of hope and consumed with a lot of sadness, Edward."

Edward snorted, "We can't help it! She is the only one who can help us . . . and why are you transforming yourself into a baby, Judy. You know she can't see you now, right! It a-i-n'-t-f-u-n-n-y . . ."

Edward glared at Judy who had already converted into a baby that made some babbling noises. Her skin was translucent and lumpy, with masses of fat on the arms, like a baby elephant. The face was squished up and pink.

The windows behind inside the room were big and had let in too much bright light from the evening sky. It bounced off the table and its light shone on the bookshelf.

Edward saw Judy crawl around the room, whilst I sat on the carpet floor leaning on my bed side wall. He saw Judy watch me intently.

Edward jutted his hand up in a half-wave and walked over towards Judy. He sat down across from her and put his hands in his lap. They were sticky with Judy's saliva. He tried to air them out. But she was being playful that she gurgled continuously making him laugh.

The moment of silence I lived in at that moment resembled a tone of a mourning feeling where one was yearning to solve a mystery and the other two were the culprit of a mischievous playtime.

# CHAPTER 18

# The Dancing Candle

The early morning sunrise was fascinating as the rays of light beam on my face. Feeling the chills on and off was just a way my body reacted to the unwanted acts. Breaking out into a cold sweat and feeling my hair damp indicated I needed a cold shower.

I had washed my hair before breakfast and sat drinking coffee in a pink turban, with a bright wet curl stamped on each cheek. It had been a while since I even heard from mom. Something seemed to change the fact that I even had a family back home.

The urge to share the canny events here was certainly frightening and would worry my parents. Remembering moments of having breakfast with them was nostalgic. It was so delicious to have an excuse for eating at the café, and besides, mom loved having to arrange things. She always felt she could do it so much better than anybody else. Oh, I miss the café.

And what a beautiful morning! Got to definitely get hold of myself from the sneaky beasts.

Coffee simply does the magic to awaken a sleepy soul. It was time to project the unpredictable situations as staying here will never be easy and the flirtatious gestures of Dominic were not making it easier. Every moment felt like a magnetic pull towards him.

Going through these fluttering thoughts certainly got me to leap up and get dressed up for my class. It was time to allow the six new candidates to attend an academic journey which was learnt in spirit and assignments would surely be conducted with their self created *'Ghost Computer.'*

I wonder what that would look like and whether it would even function or not . . . what about the printer or scanner. Do ghost lands accommodate those things? Are they even high-tech? Does it even know anything about technology?

Hmm . . . time will tell. Oh . . . that mirror—what could possibly behind it? I better see how I can find that out later today.

Humming to a random tune and putting on an elegant maroon suit certainly brightened the moment hushing the events that I went through last night. Even though I was being pretentious, that projection motivated me to get back to the classroom.

Putting on my black crystal studded hair band, I picked up my lappy and made my way to the school.

Walking past some trees were soothing. They were so exquisite, with their broad, gleaming leaves, and their clusters of orange fruit. They were like trees you envision growing on an island, solitary, lifting their leaves and fruits to the sun in a kind of silent grandeur.

From a distance, I could see Dominic near a tree and feeling the leaves of it. He bent down, put his thumb and forefinger to his nose and snuffed up the smell. When I saw that gesture I forgot all about the beasts and in my wonder I saw how he cared for things like that.

The door bell rang, so I rushed toward the classroom. I could hear the rustle of Elma's long printed skirt on the stairs.

Rushing down the corridor and taking the stairs to the next level into the classroom was and effort. The beautiful day got me late.

Placing my lappy on the desk and greeting the students quickly was a start to a new lesson.

'What is it, Jude? Why are you making too much noise?'

Margarita, another student came into the classroom. "It's the florist, Miss Ashley."

'Florist! Margarita, there could be a mistake. I never called any florist.'

"No, Miss Ashley, the florist certainly asked for you. I double checked."

'Margarita—you should enroll to be a detective. Wait a minute; I shall come to the canteen.'

It was, indeed. There, on the wooden, stood a wide, shallow tray full of pots of pink lilies. No other kind—big pink flowers, wide open, radiant, and alive on bright crimson stems.

It was amazing making me wonder who they could be from.

"O-oh, Ashley!" said Dominic, and the sound was like a little moan. He crouched down as if to warm himself at that blaze of lilies. "Secret admirer, huh! For a lovely woman like you!" he winked and left the canteen holding his cup of tea.

'It's some mistake. I never ordered any flowers. Margarita—is this a prank?'

"No! I shall get going before Miss Elma starts to find me. FYI—Flowers are lovely." She giggled and left me in my lost thoughts.

Picking up the pots of pink lilies, in one of them was a short note:

*Ashley, how are the lilies?*
*We have underestimated your abilities and present you a token of appreciation.*
*Yours,*
*S.T.J.E.R.V. ;)*

Creepy! Can flowers be delivered from Ghost land? Do they have lilies? Okay . . . now this is not worth my time . . . they have started to send me flowers. I know the flowers are amazing—but—still—spirits—oh my!

Taking the flowers, I enter the classroom and see sets of popped eyes with budding questions. Ignoring that, I place the pots next to the window pane and start off to distribute worksheets for the desired lesson.

The classroom was quiet as the students were doing their quiz worksheets with keen interested of earning more credits. The silence in the room took me to a land of more questions as I was trying to solve a riddle, I must say. The ridicule behaviors of the spirits then to compensate for that—LILLIES! Of course, the bribe was tempting.

It seemed like I was strolling down the garden and looking from a distance at a group of students trying to peep at each other's papers.

'Ahem—ahem. No peeping.'

Giggles and tease amongst the students loosened up the atmosphere of the room. As I see the pots of lilies, each pink lily was to die for. Even though it seemed to mock me, it was radiant and rejuvenating.

Touching the petals of the lilies, I hear whispers. Moving away my hand with surprise I begin to see a faint paint like image of each spirit on the petal. Each image camouflaged with the colors of the lily. Looking so appealing—yet so frightening that the beauty of the flower began to seem fake.

Each face was clearer and the flower dancing along with the tune of the light breeze through the window pane.

A bright light shone on the flowers creating this aura of mystic colors. "Today, we have no intentions to frighten you. We are giving you a sneak peak of how we can even be nice," said Thomas with a smirk.

"Yup, once in a while we can be kind too," interrupted Viera.

It was unbelievable to see how paint like faces could be seen clearly and they were actually speaking to me dancing along with the movement of the flowers.

For a change, I did not scream. I was frightened but did not scream.

"I am done," distracted Jude.

'Alright class, you may leave if you have finished and I shall post the quiz grades online later.'

"Nice lilies, Miss Ashley," said Jude with a smile.

'Thanks, they are lovely. Now you may leave. You're distracting others.'

"Sure, have a nice day." Jude left.

As I turned back to look at the flowers, the paint like faces had disappeared. Left were the flowers to add splendor to the classroom. From a distance it reflected a fine art of oil painting.

Students had completed their quiz and time was ticking as I was feeling restless wondering what could possibly be behind that mirror.

After contemplating whether I should go back to the hall or not, I decided to keep my stuff at the teacher's lounge and go to the hall where we had the luncheon. There could not be anymore procrastination since the little beasts would not be nice forever.

Making an excuse to see antique furniture for a class project was the only thing that popped up in my mind at that moment. Luckily the dining hall door was not locked and there were some cleaners inside that let me in.

Hmm . . . walking back in this hall felt different. This time it was not the attractive furniture, lighting, nor the gorgeous mirror. It was simply a research where I was a victim.

Pacing slowly halfway toward the dining hall there was this big French designed mirror. The oval shaped mirror embedded with sparkling crystals was not hard to miss. Seeing the name Roy carved on it reminded me of something behind the mirror.

How on earth can I carry this mirror out of the wall? It is hung so well and seems pretty heavy.

Oh well, there is no time to wait, I better think of something real quick—think Ashley think!

Taking one of the dining chairs, placing it in front of the mirror, I stood on it slowly holding the mirror and carefully pulling it out of the hook from which the chain was clung to. Damn—this is heavy.

I could hear a drilling sound. It was getting louder and louder, dust was rising everywhere as I placed the mirror on the floor. The spirits were howling and cheering. But I could see no one. Ignoring the cheering sound, I managed to turn the mirror around—Oh my!

The design of the mirror in front was different from the one behind as if there were two mirrors attached to it. The name Roy was also carved behind, but this time it was engraved on a shell.

I quickly clicked the picture and slid the phone into my pocket.

"ASHLEY! What are you doing here? Why is the mirror off the hook?" said Principal Orchestra crisply.

'Oh shit—shit—shit. Sorry—P—r—i—n—c—ipal Orchestra. I was looking at the antique mirror closely for a class project.'

I was so nervous and hoping the mirror wouldn't slip off my sweaty hands. Placing the mirror back into position, I was seriously spooked.

Her eyes—my heart was pounding so hard it made my chest hurt. I strained my ears in the silence that tripped over hitting a chair. A voice inside me leaped in fright. Run Ashley!

# CHAPTER 19

# The Family Inheritance

Her eyes—the principal's eyes change color from hazel to green. 'Umm—are you okay—principal? What's wrong?'

"There is nothing wrong Ashley. Simply stay away from that mirror and NEVER touch it again. Better you leave back to your work," said Principal Orchestra harshly.

Shudders ran up my spine at the sound of that atrocious voice. I huddled up against the chairs, wanting something firm at my back. And I looked up into the glowing green eyes as if she was possessed or probably going to cast a spell. I knew it, something was wrong with her. She always seemed strange.

I ran a few steps out of the house, tripped and fell over, knocking my head on a sharp stone, and I felt blood pouring from my scalp. I rolled and fell into a deep swamp. I plunged underneath the water, threshing desperately against ropelike grasses that tried to keep me down. My head finally burst out of the water, and I panted desperately for air. I could hear her laugh in the mist.

She is a witch—witch—Oh goodness—is that what Roy was hinting about or was it something else.

Her voice began to get softer and she came out of the dining hall. Our eye contact was back to normal and her eyes were hazel again.

My head started to spin with pain from my bleeding skull. I was vaguely aware that I kept trying to make my way to the edge of the swamp, but the effort was too much for my suddenly heavy limbs, until she offered her hand.

"Are you okay?" she asked with concern.

'NO! My scalp is bleeding and it hurts . . .'

"Let's take you to the clinic—ASAP."

I didn't want to be near her at all. Where was that creepy person? She seems so normal like nothing even happened.

The transparent skin on her arms swung with the thrust of her tiny motions.

'Thank you,' I responded politely, not knowing what else to say. For some reason—she was being kind and too sweet again.

The mystery was getting more complicated.

Walking slowly toward the clinic leaning on Principal Orchestra's shoulder was a risk I had to take.

The giddy feeling was certainly getting stronger as I puked on the clinic's floor.

The next moment, "Sorry . . . how do you feel now," said Dominic with empathy.

'How did I get on the bed? Did I faint?'

"Yes, you did in my arms."

'Umm . . .'

"Relax; you seem to be too stressed. Principal Orchestra mentioned she found you fallen into a swamp out of the house. What were you even doing there, Ashley?"

'What are you even doing here, Dominic?'

"Even when you are sick—you are still dominating. But you are still charming."

'You don't seem to know when to stop—even when a person is sick. Ouch, my head.'

"You were bleeding; the nurse has put the dressing. There is nothing serious. By the way, I had come into a clinic to get some pain killers when you collapsed in my arms," Dominic said and winked. He added, "You have a serious problem I presume. When you feel better, if you want to talk about it, I am here."

'Why do even care? This school is possessed, principal is possessed, god knows who else is possessed, Dominic!'

"Don't cry, Ashley. Why are you speaking that way? What did you see?"

The warmth of his hands on my waist and him tilting his weight on me to embrace me sent shivers to my body. He stroked my damp face, feeling oddly protective kissing my forehead.

As passion receded and left a sensuous dreaminess in its place. His kiss spoke expressively of being concerned. I did not want him to stop hugging me.

'Stop, Dominic. Please.'

"It's okay Ashley. Don't get paranoid. We need to talk about your hallucination. You tend to see things beneath the surface and the outcome is rather surprising. I can also feel the discomfort when I come closer to you. My intention is purely friendship and there is something about you that makes me want to care for you, so stop getting edgy."

'I am not edgy for no reason. There is no hallucination of any kind. What I am seeing or feeling is purely the truth. Yes, I should rest and I need to be alone. Thanks for being a friend. About my discomfort—umm . . . well . . . nevermind . . . please leave and thanks.'

"Alright, I shall see you later. I know your head must be aching and you are attempting to make sense of all the scenarios you are encountering. Will come check on you at the apartment."

'What scenarios Dominic! Wait . . .'

He left. His statement to that was rather absurd as he knew nothing about the spirits nor anything I went through since I arrived at this beastly school. But there is something he knows that I don't.

Aaaahhhh! My head! Rest Ashley—echoes in my mind.

The living room was shadowy, except for some light gleaming out of the muted television set. Being back in my room was heaven. There was nothing like being back into one's own home. This had become home to me where I could lay low and spend my serene time figuring out moments of horror.

The headache had become slightly better that I managed to make a cup of coffee to relax. Caffeine was very much needed in my system to process about the possessed.

The principal had shocked me and I wonder how I could face her ever again. However, I needed to get into the root of this cause. What was the connection between the principal—mirror—Roy. This had intertwined and muddled my system.

While sipping coffee I check the poem written behind the mirror. The entire poem had some sort of meaning as if the principal was some sort of Wiccan. The fragrance of a candle is definitely aromatic and can be a magical retreat. Hmm . . . well . . . surrender, justice, and heal brings about some other thought. Is she some kind of black magic expert? There are so many things to find out.

What's the relationship between Roy and Principal Orchestra? There has to be something.

I tripped over my shoes on my way to the sink to fill more water for another cup of coffee. I looked down at them allegedly, as if anyone but me could have put them there. I looked up after kicking them across the pantry and that was when I heard a knock on the door. 'Oh boy it must be Dominic.'

I poured hot water into my cup and paced to open the door. It was no surprise; Dominic had arrived bringing with him some tuna sandwiches and French fries.

'What a delight, I am starving. I was making another cup of coffee, would you like some D.'

"You seem to be in a better mood now. No hallucination. Yes please, a cup of coffee with you would be a delight. It so good to see you get annoyed. So, how is your headache now?"

'Slightly better. Still hurts, the pain killers and caffeine is doing the trick. Thanks for bringing in some food. I guess we can have dinner together. I shall also heat the chicken curry puff I bought yesterday evening. And thanks for being concerned. I guess I have to get used to the fact I have someone to annoy me here. Why don't you have a seat while I put this in the pantry.'

He sat with me while I emailed my parents and he was going through his phone. Rather he seemed like he wanted to talk about something.

'Is there a problem? You're scrolling down your phone several times with a frown.'

"Now you're being observant. No biggy—well, actually my fiancé and I have been out of touch lately."

'Out of touch—she busy?'

"To cut it short and not narrate a story—we are having problems. Or let's say she doesn't see any spark in this anymore. She asked if we could break up."

Break up! Break up! Okay he is going to be single—or he is single—single man in my room now. I am already so restless when he is around. What should I do now? SOS!

'Aah okay. Sorry to hear that. It's up to you to narrate it or not. So what is your decision?'

"Decision! She has made the decision. We are not kids. She feels no spark—countless arguments for weeks—so better break up—if that is what makes her happy. I would always care for her. I see this not going anywhere either. We have not met for almost a year. And she sees no spark . . . sorry Ashley, I am quite annoyed. Anyway, everything will be alright as days pass by. I wanted to hear your story about what you said earlier about the school being possessed."

'You're surely pissed, who wouldn't be. I have been there done that. Time and change heals it but also brings about a new set of problems. I mean to say, nothing is so calm and steady. About the school being possessed, seriously I sense something strange everywhere. Haven't you? Is there something I don't know? You even mentioned about me going through some incidents when I never mentioned anything to you. I feel there is something huge I am missing here. Please do tell.'

"Every day since I have been living here, there has been a white swirling mixture of ground and sky. I felt nothing like adrenaline or terror. Or that feeling when your heart beats so fast it makes you want to throw up. Nothing like that happened. In fact, I learned that our principal was different. She was intuitive and did have a lot of knowledge about black magic and voodoo."

'Black magic and voodoo! That's scary Dominic.'

"Yes, it is. Well no one has ever caught her doing it but some teachers have seen her acting strange . . ."

'I have—I mean—her eyes turned from hazel to green. Her voice! It was because of her I fell into the swamp.

"What really! Are you sure? Or was it some mistake Ashley?"

'Why would I even doubt it? Everything is freaky here. I have something to confide in and there is no need to say I was being dramatic. This is no fantasy but serious business.'

"Sure, tell me."

'I will tell you, but first tell me if you know anything about Principal Orchestra and this kid Roy.'

"Roy! Who is he?"

'Do you know anything about the mirror in the dining hall?'

"Well, there is one which she mentioned she inherited years ago. She insisted no one to ever go near it or touch it. There is also a sign there—don't touch the mirror."

'Really, a sign. I saw no sign. Where was it?'

"It's below on the right side. So you touched it and . . ."

'Yes, I touched and removed it off the hook.'

"You did what! No wonder her eyes changed from hazel to green. You're sneaky."

'This is not funny. Her eyes literally changed color and she got into this split personality function I supposed. I saw the mirror from close and it is surely an antique beauty. There was a message behind it. Here take a look, I took the pic through my phone before she caught me red handed.'

"You're one brave woman. Oh, it's beautiful. The poem is great. The dancing candle surely portrays her nature. I mean something to do with her and black magic. I believe she is a Wiccan or some sort of witch. She doesn't seem evil as she has always been too nice to everyone. But who knows this school is under some sort of spell. This school is everything to her."

'Okay, do you see that name down there carved—Roy? I was asking about that.'

"No, I don't know but we can find out. I can help you. But why is all this such a concern to you. It's not even your business."

'It is my business. I have to get that mirror. Roy wants it back!'

"What!"

'Umm.'

"What are you hiding?"

'Ghosts.'

"You're hiding ghosts. Where, here? How is that possible?"

'I am not hiding them. But they are always around me.'

"Them! Who is—them. Are you getting retarded?"

'I am not crazy! I am serious Dominic, there are six spirits!'

"Really? You can see ghosts—spirits—whatever. Do you practice black magic?"

'Hell no! I have been going through series of incidents and they were really spirits.'

"No wonder, that day you said—Ghosts."

'Yes! So what do I do now?'

"Well, I know and have heard of people seeing ghosts or sometimes a person is a chosen one to bring justice to a spirit. Is that your problem?"

'Yes! I am a victim of their last wishes.'

"This can't be more interesting. You see ghosts, you're the chosen one, and—oh . . . do you know their names?"

'You are finding all this amusing. Dominic, this is really serious and they can be harmful, scary, and threatening. Even though they may seem innocent, they can be quite cheeky.'

"Why are your eyes teary? I believe you. This is all new to me. What are their names?"

'Sarah, Thomas, Roy, Viera, Judy, and Edward are six teenage spirits.'

"Wow! What do they even want?"

'For now, let's say, Roy wants the mirror back. I need to know the connection between them.'

"She is my aunt!"

'Roy! You're here!'

"You see Roy, Ashley? This is getting creepy. Should I run, alert me."

'Dominic, you don't have to run. And Roy, where are you? How is she your aunt?'

"She is my dad's friend's wife. Meaning, my dad's sister married his friend's brother. She was very angry and upset with my dad when he killed her husband's brother. Since then, she has been very angry and full of vengeance. The mirror is the last thing we owned and she stole it from my mom."

'Okay! So what you want me to do. Tell her, I know Roy, hand in me the mirror. This is getting mad, completely mad. She is scary, Roy!'

"I know. She practices all sorts of black magic and has strong sense of sixth sense."

'Couldn't you tell me that earlier?'

"No I couldn't. You experienced it so now you know better. Just bring me back the mirror. It's our honor and belongs to ME."

'God damn these ghosts. They cannot order me around. And there he simply speaks and vanishes. I couldn't even see him nor say anything.'

"Ashley, I could neither hear nor see him. I could only see and hear you speak out loud. So what's the issue?"

'The mirror is a family inheritance and Roy wants it back. Orchestra stole it! I don't know how I am going to do this. But I need to find a way. I am also concerned that after each spirit has been granted his or her wish would they leave me alone or would they kill me? I am terrified, Dominic.'

"Don't worry, what come may, I am here for you. Now helping you fight this would also be my mission."

'Your mission! What's that supposed to mean?'

"In time you would know what I meant. At the moment, I just know I like to spend time with you and you're a nice person. So there is no need to dissect this relationship. You are not a victim here."

'You and your words! Fine, I won't dissect this relationship. Thank you, I really—really need to solve this mystery of chains.'

## CHAPTER 20

# The Sneaky Beasts

Our chat lasted for hours that Dominic ended up sleeping on my sofa. Stretching away from my bed, all at once I see these six faces.

'Oh you sneaky rascals! You guys are sneaky beasts.'

"Who are you talking to, Ashley? Your voice woke me up."

'The spirits are here.'

"I better leave you with them. I have a class to see to while you have your chit chat with them. Remember, everything will be okay and you don't have to get down off your bed. I shall leave."

'Bye then. See you later, D.'

Judy and Viera were staring, and those eyebrows arching up asking me several questions. 'Don't even start—you girls. I have not forgotten about you all.'

"We know!" said Edward with a smile and added, "We won't let you forget."

'Why are you all even here? I can't even run away.'

Shaking his head, "We don't mean to pry but something has to be done to solve our existence right here and this is definitely a wrong time. Being a wondering spirit is making me so angry," said Edward with sarcasm.

'What do you really want Edward?'

"Ashley! What I really want is to experience a real classroom! I want to be around real people for a while! They don't have this fear they would be killed every time because of their parents!

I want a ceremonial liberation from the sudden death. I was killed and left like a piece of shit!" He smiled modestly.

Patting Edward's back, "Yes Ashley, I wish the same. We are no dirt that everyone forgot about. The officials came and destroyed everything. I don't even know how I got here. I never felt the salvation. My soul has been wondering around until I met everyone right here at the school one day. After waiting for many years, you have come by and now you will fight for us," spoke Judy with confidence.

'Now that is an update to the network I had created. What about you Viera? What do you want—your wish? I can't believe I am here to solve dead people's wishes. Wonder if this is an honorary tribute or falling into the fire embracing my death.'

Viera simpered, Judy grinned, Sarah looked down, and Thomas refused to catch her eye. Of course, they were oblivious to their collective nature, each thought the only recipient of their attentions—these spirits didn't boast about their abilities and capabilities of harm they can bring. I could never have get away with it if I don't manage to give them what they want. I could just be where they are if things turn around.

"I have never waxed before! I wish I could experience the modern generation's way of being cool and fashionable," blurted Sarah.

"Seriously, you want to wax! Is that gonna solve your problem in being liberated, Sarah," teased Roy.

"Actually, I can see your moustache. I do wish you waxed. Smooth skin would be much easier to transmute in a young man's imagination, especially with his eyes closed," grinned Roy.

Sarah smacked Roy's head and the chuckles of the six sneaky beasts echoed my cozy room. Who could tell I was actually socializing with dead people and they could actually have a sense of humor.

Edward was thinking about what scam to operate so he can cease to conquer the classroom. He was quite keen to attend the classroom and study along with the rest of the students.

Judy and Sarah cheered for it and were thinking of various ways to enter the classroom and indulge themselves into the current education system. They opted to study what they wanted to study and their self study motto was just driving me nuts.

'Ok, you guys can make your exit while I get going to work. I need my privacy and cannot afford to spend any time with you. About sneaking into classroom why don't you guys attend Dominic's class? Go study Physics and Chemistry today. See how that goes and tell me later. Be quiet and no magical tricks there, I am serious about this. If I hear or smell anything not right—go find someone else to finish your dirty game. Now shoo—shoo—disperse!'

The smirk on their faces did confirm that they would behave for a change and one by one each evaporated like steam in air. What was seen in movies was seen in person and it was very tough to accept the phenomenon of superficial magic of dead people.

"Good morning, may I speak to Miss Ashley Preston, please?"

'Speaking.'

The voice was bright, conveying masculine bubbliness.

The voice was familiar and seemed like the man had a bad cold. His huskiness and tone sent a vibe of some kind of excitement to chat.

'OMG! Edwin—is that you—Edwin!'

"You recognized my voice even after the bad cold. It has been a while since we chatted. How are you?"

'Yes! I am glad you called. It was so unexpected. I have just so much to tell you. Where do I start—umm—how are you?'

"I am fine, Ashley. Was thinking about you, so called, remember we are still friends. How are you?"

'I know, Edwin. I am ok—living. Actually, whatever we talked about or let's say you teased me about spirits—is true.'

"It's Africa! No discrimination—it's just history and all the voodoos and black magic. So much happens there."

'Talking about voodoo, I think my principal practices it. I am finding a way to catch her red handed. Also, don't laugh! But—I—um—can see spirits.'

There was a pause, "Really! Seriously, marvelous! I knew you had some sort of talent when you encountered strange things as an archeologist."

'How come you never said anything when we were engaged or dating? I never knew or recognized anything. This is so not funny but scary Edwin. There is so much to say but I will when I visit back during the holidays. I am glad you called and do keep in touch . . .'

"I am quite pleased to do that and stay away from trouble my lady. You seem tough but who can fight spirits. They are unique and anyone can go mental with this."

Biting my lip, how could I tell Edwin—I am actually in this silly mission and I feel caged. 'Yes, who can fight with spirits? Anyway, I got to go and have a class to teach. It was nice hearing from you. Would have liked to chat more but work is sucking up. We shall Skype in a few days. Take care, Edwin."

Who would know more than I that one can go mental with spirits and more than that their super powers is beyond anyone's understanding. I cannot comprehend it. I feel like an amateur being trained in a ghost field fulfilling each spirit's wish and having this check list is insane.

Oh it's time for a hot shower and leave to a new class today.

An hour later, I walk along the corridor towards my classroom. I see a field of grass and it tempts me to lay on it. I wanted to feel the warmth and inhale the fresh fragrance of soil. How silly I would look if students' saw me. Then I remembered that I had told the spirit jing-bang to attend Dominic's class. Would they have listened to me? I should somehow take a peek later at his class.

Glancing at my watch, I enter my classroom. Everything seemed pleasant and the lesson went on well without and mischief of some sort.

The thrill and fear was killing me to find out if the spirits had attended the class or not. So I walked down the stairs and peeped from the window watching Dominic teaching. Awww—he looked adorable.

To my surprise the six sneaky beasts where in the class and were attentive when Dominic was teaching Physics.

For a moment the interior of the classroom distracted me. His room was more like a writing room in some five star cruise. The room was decorated in an Arabian style with a carved Cairo curtain. There was a huge bow window painted in white and furnished very elegantly. The room was filled with chestnut color furniture and silk curtains hanging on the side.

The ambience of the room brought about an ancient era of elite lifestyle. The chairs, shelves, lighting was bright making it feel awesome to be part of a classroom like that, especially if the teacher was Dominic.

Viera's expression amused my pondering thoughts. She stared, hypnotized with horror. She slid out of the door and was standing beside me.

She was furious. Her thoughts swiveled round the giantess like sparrows caught in a storm. "It would be better if studying was a piece of cake," she muttered.

Giggling, "You are actually spying on us," said Viera.

'I am making use of my talent, Viera. Why are you here? You got to be in there and you can't quit.'

As I glance back in the classroom, there was something very satisfying in the moment when I thrust the tip of my pen into Viera's heart during our chat to catch her attention. I watched the boys fall to the ground with the satisfaction of a job well done. It was clearly shown that Roy, Edward, and Thomas enjoyed the class. It just made me want to create a checklist where I could tick—mission accomplish for their first class, whilst Sarah and

Judy were not so fascinated but seemed moderate about their first learning experience.

When Dominic was handing in worksheets to the students, he noticed me standing outside the class. He smiled and nodded his head. Behind him was Thomas who was making funny facial expressions teasing me with him. On his left side Roy and Edward were cracking up making me feel awkward that I decided to leave the area.

"What you thinking, Ashley?" screamed Edward.

'Goodness, you frightened me. When did you guys even come out? Phew, whatever, you—GUYS. Sucks. So how was the class?'

"It was pleasant—Physics is what we are—we are the reaction of a crazy cause," said Sarah with a genial smile.

'Don't tell me you guys are not attending his next class—Chemistry! Instead of finding Physics in your existence now, it's time for some chemical reaction. Go learn!'

"I like you! You have kind off gotten to know how we are tuned," spoke Judy with a smirk.

"We shall take a stroll around and head to his next class. Hoping Dominic won't be too boring again," grumbled Viera.

'Alright sneaky beasts—time to leave me alone. I feel like a lunatic speaking alone. Now GO!'

It was such a relief seeing them leave as I wanted to nibble a bite and have a cup of tea in the cafeteria.

With that weeks passed by, and the sneaky beasts attended various classes to soothe their soul and tempting curiosity of studying in a classroom. They sneaked around, played pranks, and even burst into laughter bringing a life back within their dark world.

## CHAPTER 21

# The Mirror

'Your drunk, Dominic. What you doing here at this time of the night? Go back to your room and sleep it off. It is scary to see you like this.'

I couldn't believe he was actually drunk and was knocking on my door continuously at 3:00am.

"I am coming in! It's over Ashley. Now it is completely over!"

'What's over Dominic! What's wrong?'

"We broke up for good. Can you imagine this? Skype! You Skype and then it's so simple to break up! I am sorry, I barged in like this. I had to let it out!"

'I am sorry to hear that. Umm—so—what—now—I—mean—would you like a cup of coffee?'

"Don't be ridiculous! I am pissed off—literally sad—offer me ALCOHOL—and your asking me—COFFEE!"

I just wanted to laugh at his expressions but he seemed even more handsome and charming when he was sad, torn and lost. 'No alcohol, only coffee! Where would I get alcohol from? Sit and whine. Wait I shall bring coffee.'

After having pouring coffee, I could see him conquering my bed. He was whining, "You're so BITCHY! Heartless! Fine—Go! I am not alone! I have—I have—found someone too."

I froze as I could feel my heart pounding and hoping he would not say my name or anyone else's name like that—drunk! He was silent and I patted his shoulder.

'Dominic—coffee!'

He got up and was quite sloppy as he put his legs down the bed and sat up straight leaning on the pillows. "Seriously! Coffee. That's not what people should drink when they break up. Its sucky, unhealthy and completely an off track drink. But you made it—so . . ."

Gulp, "It's tasty."

'Is it? Break up sucks! I know it does—well, I am no good for you at this situation, but you can whine, scream, and have another cup of coffee to see the bright side of your life.'

"My bright side is—Y—O—U."

Looking into his eyes intently, I felt my mouth dry and moved a few steps backwards to sit on the sofa. Dominic sipped his coffee in silence and asked for another cup. He listened, surprisingly.

Making another cup, I sat back on the sofa. Dominic vented and I could feel his warm hand around me as he sat beside me. Thanking away, he doses off on my shoulder. I slowly and comfortingly move away placing his head on a cushion and sit on my bed.

Watching him sleep peacefully and his silent battle in his mind portrayed an innocent child. It was quite sad to see his heart break. He was shattered. Love and its consequences, some use people, some choose career over love, some lose hope, and some are just victims of fate. God knows what was next. For now all I could think was how to get that mirror back from the dining hall. After seeing a glimpse of Principal Orchestra's scary side it was all getting more difficult. I wonder how I would manage it. But looking at Dominic, I knew I found a good friend and he would surely come up with something.

The loud sound of yawn woke me up. Dominic was coughing and yawning. His sound effects echoed the entire room that I had to wake up.

'Are you ok?'

"Yes! I have a hangover. Your coffee didn't help. But thanks you gave it anyway. I should get going before anyone spots me out of your room. There would be trouble of unethical crap. So now or let's say today is a new day—I am officially throwing this ring away and single. Feels light a burden is off . . ."

'Burden! Just because it hit your ego and sadly its over don't say burden.'

He came over and leaned on the bed and kissed my forehead, "You have been a good buddy! See you later."

He kissed my forehead, that kiss—goodness. He is gone now—focus—MIRROR—no Dominic.

That sensation was soothing yet restless. I had to get off the bed and have a cup of coffee. Knowing I had no class this morning, it was better to find a way to get that Mirror.

Presuming she was a Wiccan, I was wondering if there was something more to her story.

Getting back to that dining room would not be easy anymore. Hmm, perhaps I have to ask someone for help. Who would that be?

Jude and Dominic could be of some help. Those two owe me big time. So I better start to get ready. The aroma of the coffee was simply out of this world on a tiring start of a day.

All at once, the temperature around me plunged. I froze in place, suddenly petrified, as someone moaned in terror from the other side of the school. The sound scraped my nerves raw as I heard a siren's sound and some kids shouting, "Fire, Fire!"

When I turned around I could see smoke had engulfed the air and it was blurry. The pungent smell was making it hard to breathe. Pacing towards the area, I realized it was near the dining hall. The fire had taken place as a student had played a prank by burning his friend's books out of revenge of some sort.

Oh these kids and WOW I didn't have to do anything much. I need to find Dominic to see how I can get that mirror out of the dining hall.

He was not found anywhere until I saw him at the cafeteria sipping something. 'Dominic, hey—come here please.'

"Hey, why are you whispering? Ashley."

'Remember, I told you about the mirror in the dining hall, I need to get that out of there. I have to—it's a demand or let's say life and death kinda thing. Help me get it out, so I can hand it to Roy.'

"Whose Roy?"

'That spirit ghost I told you about.'

"Seriously, now we are gonna start stealing for dead people. What's gotten into you? Don't give me that look."

'Just come with me—Please.'

"Fine, let's get going, Orchestra is not around."

'Thanks.'

The scene outside the dining hall building was under control so we sneaked into the magnificent and well decorated room again.

"This room is certainly something. It's so cool and look at all these artifacts. Orchestra has good taste or perhaps it's the person who built the school."

'Stop admiring the art work, look there is the mirror. Amazing isn't it. Wait I shall show you the poem carved into the second mirror behind it.'

"You look so excited. LOL, Ashley, has the spirit gotten you mad. Oh shoot! That is cool. Beautiful carving! Wait, let me take a pic and see what we should do with candles. Perhaps there is a way to do this—maybe—chanting every line and lighting candles would bring peace to your Roy."

'He is not my Roy! And—umm . . . maybe you're right, if we take the mirror and chant this and lighting a few candles, perhaps it would bring peace to Roy. You want to try it? We need to find candles.'

"This is insane—I don't chant stuff—random stuff."

'Me too—my first time.'

"You are too cute—fine—wait, let me find candles."

Dominic was searching for candles and pointed out two pink candles on the candle stand placed on the dining table.

"You have a lighter? Ok wait—will check in the kitchen." Lighting the two candles, he brought them and placed it on the ground in front of the other mirror.

Having to chant every line of the poem was beginning to get creepy.

Saying each word softly and with purity was what I really wanted to do for Roy. Hoping it worked.

*Aromatic luminescence*
*Magical retreat*
*Soul sparks*
*Wax melting*
*Mind clearing ways*
*Flame swaying*
*Cleansing*
*Inviting love and light*
*Awaken the ignorant mind*
*Dazzling gracefully*
*A ballerina*
*Carefree*
*Romantic encounter*
*Kiss to the nature*
*Surrender*
*Yummy chemistry*
*Justice*
*Heal*

Dominic was swaying his head closing his eyes as if we were about to do some magic. It was getting amusing. After chanting the poem five times continuously to see if anything would happen. Dominic heard a scream and to our surprise we could see the flame rising slowly. Now it was getting haunting.

Strange voices were heard. The sound of the breeze was getting louder. I took the mirror and was ready to leave the dining hall until Orchestra was standing in front of us with her eyes changing to green.

Dominic held my hand and took the mirror from me.

Orchestra did not notice her flaming clothes until the fire had burnt through the heavy silk of her skirt and began to scorch her skin. Leaping up in terror, Orchestra threw her lamp over the flames. She was not scared anymore; she fled into the dining hall as the flames engulfed her body.

Slowly, everything changed. She was not Principal Orchestra.

She had transformed to something I had no words for.

I could not tell from the way her body was engulfed in fire and slowly her human like features were changing.

She was attacked by many butterflies, more and more butterflies appeared of various colors. Soon, they vanished and her green eyes were prominent as the fire had subsided. One could easily tell that magic was flowing through her entire body cells as she lifted her right index finger towards me.

"You! What have you done! The mirror is my heritage and NO ONE can come near it. You have broken the SPELL and awakened the souls of my family."

'What the fuck!'

"Principal Orchestra, Umm—we have not done anything, actually enlighten me?"

"Get out of here DOMINIC! SHE—SHE—CAN—SEE—him—Yes you can! Tell me, what have you come here to destroy and take away?"

"She looks grisly; her hair knotted, and watch her simian eyes. Scary! What a sudden change!" said Dominic in fear.

'Stop it Dominic. She can hear you. And stop whispering. Is she gonna kill me?'

"I dunno! How should we escape, Ashley?"

'I DON'T KNOW! We have broken the spell and now we know she is a witch and casts spells, what we need to know is how should we get rid of her and bring Roy the mirror.'

"Yup, why don't you read the poem again—chant it? Let's see what happens."

Reading every line of the poem with my true heart only to bring justice to Roy was my motto. I could feel a soft tingly energy around me and seeing Roy appear was getting the entire scenario intense.

'What you doing here, Roy?'

"I had to come now. Our souls have been sucked into this room and . . ."

"Oh you little brat—ROY! Because of your father my husband's brother died. Then we lost everything because of the blood feud. Disgusting! He died in this very room many years ago and today this silly and crazy woman he unveiled the doors of pain and darkness," interrupted Orchestra with her raspy voice.

"Don't you blame and claim things you are ignorant about! Ashley, is here to help bring me liberation, set me free and not what you think and want to do. It is because of you I am here. This mirror has to be taken away. Our life is being seized here and all of us need to be set free!" said Roy with a fuming and rasping voice.

He added crisply, "Ashley! Her power lies behind the second mirror with the poem. If you can destroy that she sets ME and my family free. It is because of her black magic and dark power we are all rusting and suffocating here. Take the mirror from Dominic! GO! Quick!"

My hand trembling as I take the mirror off Dominic's hands. Orchestra comes closer and with a strong force she pushes me. The mirror is broken into two. Dominic rushed to get the mirror with the poem on it as Roy guards the other.

'You Witch! This is not what I came here for! I came here to make my life. I began to like my job until I met these spirits! Damn! Everything has turned to one sick game. Now I want to bring Roy his right to liberation—You WITCH! Whence come those inexplicable maneuvers which change our happiness into restraints, and our dignity into hesitancy? I wake up in the finest of spirits, with a penchant to chant in my heart. And today I declare that you HAVE to end this as I shall DECLARE WAR!'

"Ashley! Oh my, you are so into this. Are you okay? Did you get hurt?" asked Dominic with distress.

Falling back on the ground because the ruthless witch was proving her power through magic, Roy slid the mirror right in time so I got hold of it and threw it towards the pillar.

The sound of the shattered glass got Orchestra to pause in silence as a steam like vapor engulfed the room. Roy was getting choked and fell flat on the ground.

"Ashley! What have you DONE? You released all the souls and—AND—AND they will be set free. This is not done yet! I shall get back to you! WAIT AND WATCH!" screamed Principal Orchestra.

Orchestra vanishes in the air like vapor and leaves all of us confused about the supernatural power of magic we got to see. The entire scene was terrifying.

Looking at Roy was very agonizing. Holding him in my arms in his physical state as tears trickling down, a cold shiver passing over my skin, has completely distressed my nerves and given me a fit of low spirits bearing in mind the forces of nature about life and death. The chirpy Roy was finally getting what he wanted. He was the first to be liberated and the sight of him leaving was not only depressing but I felt I was losing a friend.

The fear he brought, the terror he showed me, the threat he pointed all went away as I saw him nearing his true exit of his spirit life.

Tears weld up in his eyes, "Ashley, thank you, thank you, thank you. I—cannot—speak. I know—this is what—I wanted, and now—I feel I am going to leave too fast. Thank you again."

He could say no more as he continued looking at me and Dominic with empathy. Sarah, Thomas, Judy, Edward, and Viera were there to witness his last words. Holding hands tightly and letting him go was the hardest thing.

Roy slowly condensed in the air. He was gone! He was healed—he got his JUSTICE!

Dominic was stunned and said nothing. He could not utter a word as he was in denial that he got to see a spirit for the first time in his life. He sat down on the floor opposite Roy completely zapped.

Orchestra was gone, Roy was gone, and the other sneaky beasts also left.

Dominic and I were left with a gloom of suspicion as we saw the other mirror gone. It left a threat and declared a war between Orchestra and I. The next morning would be a rise of a new personality and new goals as five spirits were yet to cross over to attain their liberation.

Dominic held my hand and we exited the dining hall with pondering thoughts that only brought about fear, more questions, and curiosity.

How could I even have a peaceful SLEEP!

'Dominic, can you stay over tonight . . .'

"Yes!"

## CHAPTER 22

# Would you be my Prom Date?

Having Dominic in the room was a relief. The entire scenario of Orchestra and Roy were having reruns in my mind like an electrifying socket. Leaning on Dominic's shoulder for some sleep was not even close to a healing process, but comforted my loneness.

His warmth and support fostered my fear with courage and enabled me to wake up to another day of work. His kiss on my cheeks and a tight hug was soothing and hinted a new flame of romance of some sort. Getting carried away with his gestures and assurance of friendship was noble yet a burden to whether I could balance romance between fulfilling the spirits wish. He being with me was actually activating my eagerness to seek justice and get the matter sorted as soon as possible.

After having sorted out my clothes, I was ready to take part as a teacher without having any alarmed situation take place. Also remembering the prom night was nearing, my goal for now was getting Thomas a date. The question was—HOW? Would nature permit him to live a human life for three days? Can something magical occur where his wish comes true?

As I was rushing, I had to leave my fear, doubt, and despair behind locking the doors of soreness and headed to class.

It was eleven o'clock, when I realized that I'd left one of the textbooks upstairs on my bed. With a dramatic sigh, climbing the stairs slowly back to my room noticed the lights were faint in the long hallway, and the old boards creaked under somnolent crushed. The room was filled with an outlandish, sharp smell having me breaking out into chills. There was a strange feeling of malevolence in the room, as if a spiteful gaze were fixed upon me.

I could hear Thomas breathing on the far side of the room—a heavy sound, almost as if he had been running. He crept along the wall, "So I heard there is a prom coming up soon. Looking forward for it—and you forgot your history textbook."

'That was creepy, Thomas! Please don't ever do that again. Yesterday Roy and TODAY you are creating havoc.'

"I was just kidding around. Well—well—well—I don't care—chill Ashley! Will see you soon," said Thomas with infuriation and crept out of the window pane.

I reached out to the second shelf and took the textbook. Looking around the empty room sent out these chills as it looked empty but it hardly was. The invasion of the dark world was very well vacating in my tiny and cozy home I call it now.

Hurrying back to the school, I entered the class just in time until I spotted the crew. Viera, Judy, Edward, Sarah, and Thomas sat quietly on a bean bag that was placed near Margarita's table.

I so wished I could scream or vanish but I couldn't. Pretending to be this ideal teacher was getting so hard. The whole knowledge sharing process was sucking up my wisdom by spirits.

Margarita's hair had flopped out of place. She slowed down with her art work to adjust her hair and tie its lengths back and out of her face. A strong wind had struck up, as Thomas was blowing towards her. The windows opened and the wind had been constantly blowing about her nose and eyes until she started squinting.

Thomas needed to be spanked. In the next moment he was beside Margarita and feeling her skin on her right cheek. I began to shiver as my eyes widened with panic.

He looked at me and sat back down on the bean bag.

Margarita was scratching her cheek and later kept her art work inside her folder.

Hmm . . . what just happened? I thought. Thomas was playful but not quite a forward person. What if . . . Margarita could be his date? But how could that happen. He is a spirit—no one could see him.

All this was getting bizarre and I was lost in my thoughts while erasing the board. The prom was in a month and there were loads to do—the loads to do were only for one person—THOMAS. Aaaarrgghhh!

Calm down—Ashley! Ringing in my mind I started with the history class. The powerpoint presentation, and the video was seen. However, the discussion about the Chinese Dynasty still could not get my mind sorted out.

I felt pressured deeply that I felt my head would explode until the school bell rang for a short break.

Keeping back the projector into the bag, "Miss Ashley, I would like to update you about the prom theme. The last time we all discussed has been much progressed," updated Jude.

'Wait a minute Jude, I shall keep the projector and you can tell me what has progressed.'

"Sure. Let me help you with the projector and you can sort out other belongings."

'Someone is being extra nice and in a hurry. What's up! I smell something . . . tell my detective.'

"LOL, OMG—Hmm . . . nah . . . ah well . . . the theme for the prom this time is Magical and Mystical and it's also about the prom date."

'Interesting theme! What about the prom date?'

"I need help with that."

'You need my help? Hmm . . . who do you want to ask out?'

"Margarita."

'What! Really!'

"Why what's wrong?"

Phew, 'Nothing. Just—that's great. So how can I help?'

"I have two classes with her and I don't know her well apart from our group work and her sarcasm."

'You guys have one thing in common. Both of you are the curious types. Just like a detective. I remember when I received lilies she questioned me several times. And you questioned me about Dominic and the drug issue, remember, until when Dominic appeared and simply closed that chapter. About the prom, we still have a month and it's not too late. You have time to get to know her and ask her before someone else does. You never know you have competition—what I mean is, you never know someone also thinks the way you do. By the way what do you like about her?'

"You're right! I should *Poke* her more often on Facebook, *Retweet* her sarcasms and quotes on Twitter and probably head to the cafeteria now. What I like about her is—she is bold, witty, chirpy, and kinda cute. That's enough to take her to the prom. Thanks for listening, by the way. See you later, Miss Ashley."

'Okay then. Have a great day!'

Oh goodness, *Poke* her more often on Facebook, *Retweet* her sarcasms and quotes on Twitter. She is bold, witty, chirpy, and kinda cute. That's enough to take her to the prom. Hmm . . . I guess everyone has their choice. What on Earth should I do now? Who would Thomas go with? I should talk to him about it. At this point he was not to be seen. The crew of spirits had vanished.

Oh lord, and the theme—Magical and Mystical! I have seen enough of supernatural and witchy stuff.

I wonder what would happen next.

The next month passed down with fluidity. The mischievous spirits became good students. They attended every class and enjoyed practical assignments and hoping they had a magical computer and printer to submit their assignments. Their oral presentation with me showed their keen interest in various subjects.

With the days that passed by, the Magical and Mystical prom day was nearing. It was another four days of waiting and an evening of creative design work and middle and high school students would be looking vivacious.

Not to miss—Principal Orchestra's would probably wear her witch costume and her glare on Dominic and I in the past few days have been uncomfortable.

After that day at the dining hall, she was not to be seen nor did she try to say anything to me directly. But her two warning notes to me painted on my bathroom mirror stopped me to take any action until now. Whatever it is, the mirror has to be taken away from that crazy woman and she has to leave this school. God knows what else she was hiding.

This whole mirror and prom date scenario got Thomas no date. He was getting furious as all he wanted was to go out with Margarita.

I had enough of thinking how he would go out on a date with her. What could one do anyway; it was not a piece of cake. Leaving everyone behind, I strolled at the garden and bumped into Cooky.

"How are you Miss Ashley? It's been a while."

'Yes, Cooky, haven't seen you in months.'

"You look worried. Something!"

'Yes, something. Well . . . have a question. If a person is dying or dead and has a last wish, but if the person is a spirit how can one help that person to fulfill it.'

"You talk about dead people."

'Yes—dead people!'

"You can see dead people."

'Umm . . . not really . . . once in a while.'

"Spooky, Miss."

'Oh someone help me. Cooky thanks for listening. I shall . . .'

Someone patted my back, 'Charlie! How are you?'

"Miss, you look excited. Been sometime since we met, but I have seen you around."

'Oh okay. Yup been a while. All okay with you?'

"Yes, but maybe not with you."

'What do you mean, Charlie?'

"I saw what happened at the dining hall."

'What did you see?'

"Everything!"

'Shit! Everything here is spooky and a mystery. I need help to grant someone's wish and it is crazy difficult. My head is going to explode. Can you help?'

"I am glad I found you alone and we could talk about it. You need a heads up. There are a lot of things you're not aware of that goes around at this school. I can sense a lot of darkness around you and yes I can help. What is it? And what I saw that day, I was shocked that someone else could also feel the sensation and found out the truth about Orchestra."

'Don't talk about the woman; she is simply cunning and sweet tongued. I wonder why she has turned to this way and trying to harm or let's say guard the school for her selfish purposes. Finally all the souls are released and she is very upset with me. I am sure something bad will hit me like a dagger piercing someone's heart. I am so scared about that. I can't even leave the school—you know . . . well . . .'

"You're protected to some extent. They will make sure she doesn't harm you for their selfish purposes and they get what they want," said Cooky with assurance.

'You too, Cooky. You know?'

"Yes, we were trying to put out the fire that day. Until we heard loud sounds and fire engulfing around Orchestra. And don't forget we have been living here for years," spoke Cooky with hesitance.

'Charlie, there is this teenage spirit, his last wish is to go on a prom date and there are four days left. After his wish is being granted he will leave. The whole point is he is a spirit and how can he go out with a living person. Another problem is he wants to go with this other student Margarita when she is already going with Jude. I need a solution asap! What can you think you can do?'

"Prom date! That's his last wish, so silly. SPIRIT! Aah well, Ashley, I don't practice any sort of magical treats for dead people, but I have heard of two people who can help. I remember years ago someone mentioned about *John Mosaic* and *Barney Peacock*. But they perform intense rituals and are at this highest level where one can never even imagine," described Charlie convincingly.

'John Mosaic and Barney Peacock—their names are strange. And I am sure they can help in some way. Where do they stay?'

"In a forest which is eight hours away."

'Eight hours away. That's far and we don't have much time. What if nothing happens—then?'

"Hmm . . . I don't know the way and I got to find details so that would take a day. I have a plan. Meet today at nine for dinner after everyone is asleep and tell that spirit to be present at that point. We can think of something. I should ask Zuri. He reads a lot of these black magic books, he would know something," suggested Charlie.

'Zuri, too! Wow, this school and the people. I hadn't known for months.'

"Don't panic and see you at nine."

'Bye, Cooky and Charlie.'

They left leaving a burden of questions and got me into this worried state of mind. The entire chapter of a mysterious finding had unlocked and brought about a new hope.

For now strolling down the garden was needed and later at nine an imperative decision was to be made.

After having a word with Thomas we headed to Charlie's home and noticed that Dominic was following me.

"Where are you going at this point of time, Ashley?"

'Finding a solution—wanna come? I have no time for explanation. Just come and you shall know.'

"Of course, I will."

A good system for enlightening was yet unknown facades that consists of placing the subject in a totally new state of affairs and observing his responses as we had to find out a way to get Thomas into that prom night.

Entering Charlie's home was welcoming, he served us cheap red wine, his gestures were appreciating. The lamb steak, boiled vegetables and mash potato was average; however, his encouragement towards the knowledge of black magic was getting creepier when Zuri mentioned he could perform something that would not harm anyone, but it would be a twenty-four hours of chanting where the spirit gets what he wants and does not harm anyone.

"I am no pro in black magic as I stay away from it. I simply read and acquire knowledge about it to protect my family and friends. I do perform chants for peace and love in a manner it does not harm anyone time to time. But after hearing your entire story and feeling about Thomas around, I have accepted to perform this ritual where he gets to appear like a human for only seventy-two hours then he departs automatically, letting go of his revenge and embracing a new world of forgiveness. Does he agree? If he misuses or takes advantage of any sort, nothing happens and his soul departs without any delay for him receiving his last wish. Are you ready to take that chance?"

"Yes, I agree Ashley. The next three days of my life will be a memorable and a treasure I won't forget in many lives," confirmed Thomas with a smile.

The apprehensive feeling Dominic and I felt as we exchanged concerned looks was certainly going to be tested as we had no choice but believe in Zuri and his word.

That night a new outlook to magic would be seen, as in twenty-four hours, Thomas would get to appear like a human and attend the prom night. Now the concern was—Margarita.

Chanting had started and seventy-two candles were lit and we decided to leave Charlie's home. The entire ritual was to take place behind Charlie's yard. A tent was being built so no one would suspect. The kind charity of helping without asking anything in return was priceless and something grateful I needed was to gain liberation by releasing the spirits one by one which then would bestow me salvation.

We left and the focus on the prom was getting exciting and cheery.

The next day, Jude had mentioned that his dad was ill and he had to help in the morgue and would arrive at the prom quite late or maybe not even make it.

As much as that sounded sad, it was great news for Thomas and I. The chanting was working in some way. A ray of hope for Thomas was seen.

Tick tick one, tick tick two, twenty hours had passed by and I could see Thomas's features prominently as he lay on my bed the next evening.

The sixteen year old brown eyed teenager looked handsome. How could one reject his proposal to the prom date! Margarita would be crazy to say no.

His fair skin, chocolate hair color, and slightly toned physique depicted a passing adolescent age soon embracing his masculinity in a mature manner. What a pity, he was going to leave soon. There was no more room for him to reside as he didn't know where he belonged anymore. It was time for him to feel soulful again.

Thomas had hugged me unexpectedly and rejoiced to his new existence. He then left and enjoyed his presence around the school the next day.

This entire transition of a spirit being alive and parading around the school was thrilling and scary deep down as I had to prepare legal documents for Thomas.

Having to file some documents of him being an exchange student from England was settled. Thomas then went to the art room and introduced himself to Margarita, "Hello there. I hope I am not intruding. What is your art work on? By the way, my name is Thomas Boyle. I am new here."

Peeping from distance was so cool. This whole teenage prom thing was kind of a jaw drop moment. The look on Margarita's face was cute. For a moment she blushed and paused for a while. Her sarcasm had vanished as Thomas stood closer to her seeing her art work.

"So Thomas, umm . . . you can take a look, it's just still life of nature. Am trying to get the mountains right. Welcome to our school. My name is *Margarita Flinghead*. And how did you enter the art room without permission," spoke Margarita bashfully.

"I do have permission. I am taking art this semester and you have an interesting name. So how many Margaritas' did your parents have to get you?"

"Ah well . . . that's not funny, you—Brit boy!"

"Am kidding! Oh, just a casual question about this prom thingy. How does this whole thing work out here? Are you going to the prom?"

"Yup! Actually I was but . . ."

Before she says no I better shoot the question, thought Thomas and blurted, "Do you wanna go with me?"

Swallowing her saliva and contemplating for a few seconds, "Yes, I can. By the way, one of my friend was going with me but he got busy with some sudden situation. So if he happens to make it to the prom I would also spend time with him."

"Sure, Margarita. Could you show me around the school?"

"Yes."

Thomas and Margarita toured around the school and spent time at the cafeteria for some time updating each other about their lives. The witty young girl and the new wave back to the living world were enjoyed every moment before the prom.

Having seen them chat away and that giggle echoing was a sign of a new crush. Too bad Margarita would have to enjoy the moment for a snail time.

That night having to sleep peacefully was victorious after days. I was looking forward to see the Magical and Mystical prom night.

The exhilarating night was right here at the right time when Thomas walked into the ravishing and classic decorated room with Margarita. He was wearing a black and red tuxedo whilst Margarita wore a shaded pink georgette and silk off-shouldered sequenced dress that went with her name. She simply depicted a sweet and sour strawberry margarita. Her dark brown eyes looked at Thomas admiringly and it totally showed she had a crush on this handsome young Brit boy.

The tuxedo complimented Thomas's complexion. He paced up toward me, "Thanks, Miss Ashley. You're a really nice person. You know what I am talking about," he winked.

'Thank you very much. I'm very flattered.'

"We shall see you at the dance floor."

'Yes sure.' Everything worked out. Wow, it was simply amazing to be true. The sneaky beasts were not so beastly after all. Dominic was standing beside me watching every move like he was trying to get into my head.

He slowly came closer discreetly, "Your skin is as creamy as whipping cream. And for a change your voice is low and sweet. You smell great and you're a great company. Oh and I love your backless red suit. No one can take their eyes off you tonight. You're a lifetime of bliss for every man on this planet. So later, would you take the pleasure of a dance with me tonight?"

'My skin is creamy like whipping cream! Bliss! Your making me shy now . . . you're totally hilarious. What a tacky then aspiring compliment. And yes I would love to dance with you later, D. Hey, your charmingly kinky with your gray and black blazer.'

"Eh . . . you know Ashley, you are going to make me fall for you if you don't stop talking."

A sharp arrow of love was pierced into my heart leaving butterflies everywhere. Smiling away, I strode towards the bar for a glass of Sangria.

A couple of hours later, long after Thomas and Margarita enjoyed the roasted chicken, grilled fish, and rice, a 3-D pointed hologram with pinkish, yellow and purple highlights had appeared in the ball room.

The mystical night was surrounded by various costumes, whilst Principal Orchestra wore a blue fairy costume. She actually looked great carrying herself elegantly with hypocrisy fabricating it. Elma wore a yellow tube long flared dress. She looked charming.

The way Orchestra was glaring at me the entire evening was horrifying. She almost made me trip twice. The silent battle between us was getting intense as the night passed by. Having to ignore her and being distracted by Thomas was what I needed. Also to have his identity hidden from her was a challenge I had to meet tonight. Oh! Those horrifying eyes!

Having to party again after so long was peppy. Drinking three glasses of Sangria elevated the sugar rush and got me hyper.

Dancing with Dominic at fairy tale songs was groovy and our close contact was passionate.

'I would like some wine, Dominic. No more Sangrias"

"You know wine would be served after an hour only for the teachers and later Champagne would be popped for the prom king and queen."

'Oh, yes I forgot about it. I guess I should wait an hour and I hope Thomas and Margarita win the prom king and queen. LOL, what a gift Thomas can take to heaven.'

"You're one cheeky woman too, with a pinch of humor, beauty, wisdom, and kindness."

'I am flattered, Dominic. Look at them. Thomas looks so happy.'

I could see Thomas having that smirk towards me. His grin later reflected inner peace. He whispered something to Margarita then kissed her cheek.

Having seen him paced towards me, I stopped dancing. He stood beside me, "Would you dance with me tonight? I don't mind two prom dates. If you were younger, I would have asked you out."

'Alright flirty boy, let's have the dance.'

Dominic backed out politely and waited at the bar.

Dancing on two songs with Thomas was fun. Seeing his teary eyes, 'It's okay Thomas. I will miss you a lot. You see I have never danced with a ghost before. On top of that—you're handsome and charming. You do flirt a lot and probably if I was younger and we lived in a moment of reality I would be delighted to be your date. You've got one more day. Make the most of it. And do spend quality time with Margarita. I think she has a crush on you. Hmm . . . crush at first sight, eh.'

"Yup, I can sense that too. She is pretty. Again—thank you for everything. The prom is electrifying with many wearing different types of masks and it blends well with wizard, witches, and of course fairies. The entire theme tonight is Magical with Margarita. I can see Mister Dominic waving. I guess he wants you at the bar. Go on and will see you later."

Thomas went back to Margarita holding her hand, "You're a charming person. I will never forget you and this night. Would you show me around the school again? I can't bear to forget any moment not walking around the school with you. Shall we?"

"Sure. Why do you sound so sentimental, Thomas? Are you going anywhere? You would be here for some time, yeah? So you won't forget the school easily. But we can always go now. We also got to head back before the prom king and queen is being announced."

"We will, Margarita."

With that the prom night streamed artistically leaving memories to all as Dominic and I decided to leave back into our rooms.

The moment to be alone having neither any spirit nor a flame of seduction to distract my serene closure was a dream come true.

I looked forward for the next day, where Thomas would update me about his fairy tale experience and of course having to face his departure to a new world would be depressing.

All this portrayed a cloudy sky clearing its way for stars to shine bringing a light hearted sensation.

## CHAPTER 23

# John Mosaic and Miss Barney Peacock

What a peaceful sleep I got. Felt like I slept for ten hours even though it was for only six. It wasn't a surprise when I saw Thomas already sitting on the shelf waiting for me to wake up.

With his eyebrows gathered together and a little eager shrug of his shoulders. I realized that this was his way of courteously protesting against the unnecessary wait motioning him to proceed. He got off the shelf rapidly, as if to make up for lost time.

Finally I said, 'Well, Thomas, I want to go for a shower. But I shall not ask you to leave unless you like.' He seemed to throw himself off so quickly that he reached the ground. Then he stretched out his hands appealingly to me and implored me not to go for shower and talk.

"Last night was good. I had an amazing time at the prom. Oh, that kiss was good too. Look at your facial expression, Ashley—kiss on her cheeks! Don't think too far. When we went for a stroll, to my surprise later that night Jude came by for some time. Whatever, the prom night went . . ."

'So who was the prom king and queen?'

"I was getting there."

'Sorry, did you?'

"Nops, someone else got to be the prom king and queen. I don't care about that. The whole point was being able to live like a human and go on a date with a charming girl wearing a tuxedo during high school. I loved the moment. Thanks for that."

'That's great. So how do you feel otherwise?'

"I feel good Ashley. My numb soul has some feeling. And speaking about numbness, I feel the time is nearing soon as I speak to you the ability to be seen as human is beginning to vanish."

'I am sorry you went through a lot, Thomas. I can see that you're fading. Where are your legs? And now your body? Has it been seventy-two hours? Oh shit what's happening!'

"What's happening, Ashley? I believe I had some time left. Or was it until this morning. Does that mean I don't have much time left? Oh no . . . do tell Margarita my parents met in an accident and I had to leave back to London. Make up something."

'You're so cute . . . your concerned about her. Now I only see your head. This is insane and sad! Thomas . . .'

"I am leaving Ashley . . . thank you for everything. Bye guys! Got to go now."

'When did you guys come? All of you were so quiet.'

"We knew its time. I guess one by one, each of us would depart that way. It was beginning to be comfortable with you, Ashley," said Viera in her husky voice. She fell to her knees and burst into more tears.

'Oh lord, he's gone! Thomas left! Why am I feeling so sad? You guys have been a pain and now when each of you are leaving it should be a celebration for me, but it doesn't quite seem that way sometimes.'

I had to speak to Zuri to find out what happened. Did the entire ritual backfire? Everything was a puzzle now. Thomas was I guess in a better place and obviously it wasn't like a farewell party was to be thrown, but everything was so sudden.

I was left in the empty room to sob and sob.

Realizing the entire scenario had to come to an end, I took a cold shower to wipe away the hidden tears of joy that brought Thomas justice and he was in a better place.

Remembering about what Charlie had mentioned about John Mosaic and Barney Peacock, it became significant that I met them to find a way to destroy the other mirror Orchestra took away and how Viera, Edward, Sarah and Judy could be healed. I could not take any more of this. Everything was simply out of control and painful!

Days had passed by and the remaining four spirits attended their classes behaving like nothing had happened.

At the end of the class, I sat down to rest myself and began to look around. It struck me that it was considerably colder than it had been at the commencement of my walk. Looking upwards I noticed that great thick clouds were drafting rapidly across the sky. There were signs of a coming storm in some condescending section of the air. I was getting a little cold and there I saw Charlie walking towards his car.

'Charlie! Wait up . . . Charlie!'

"What happened? Why are you running?"

'It's about John and Barney. I want to see them. I want to know everything about them. Take this as a mission, but I have to . . . have to see them.'

"You look worried. Sure, I will find out and get back to you as soon as I can. Don't get too hard on yourself. It will be alright . . . John and Barney are ultimate healers."

'Thank you, but Orchestra has been sending me death notes. She has also threatened she would kill me if I continue to investigate about the mirror and if I continued to help some spirits. I feel squashed between two worlds—one is a cunning witch at our school and the other are the wandering spirits. All this is getting too hard to deal with . . . I . . .'

"Don't worry, Ashley. I shall find out about them and get back to you. This time this thing seems huge. Where did all these ghostly stuff come from and how to deal with is not in my caliber. We got to do something. I shall also talk to Zuri, and then we can plan to leave soon. It's his friend who knows about John and Barney," he said patting my shoulder.

'Thank you Charlie.'

Charlie left and I sat back on the grass field. All these whirlpool of thoughts came back and forth. I thought I could even come close to manage everything—work—mirror—wishes. There was this thing that had been hanging around in my mind over the years, tucked down inside of me like a lucky charm that I don't want to lose, and every now and then I take it out and admire it a little when I need something to fall back on that makes me feel like I'm not so much a loser as I sure seem to be now. Dominic, Charlie, and Zuri have been quite supportive. All I need to know now who and what are John and Barney really like.

Contemplating with that thought I went back to my room and later that night I had received a text message from Charlie that we could visit John and Barney in the weekend which was two days away.

Having to read that sent the chills signaling an opportunity to end the unwanted trauma for good bringing a silent joy. Sarah, Judy, Edward, and Viera had been around for some time and it was time they embrace the reality to leave into a new world where they were given a chance to move to a next level which I was completely unaware of but knew there was something out there.

It was just about the end of the week and I was packing my bag to meet the ultimate healers, just like what Charlie had quoted.

Dominic had come around a couple of times to confirm if I was ready to do this. His agitated behavior was hilarious. Reassuring him over and over again and making sure I won't step back was my goal. Sharing my fear with him was not what I delved for but being with him brought about an inner strength to face the entire scenario.

With that the weekend was here. Having to leave at five in the morning was weary. The silent road and Dominic's shoulder to rest on was soothing as the sound of birds chirping were rising after some time.

While Zuri's friend *Darty Bingo* was driving, Zuri shared a brief history about John Mosaic.

"Ashley, to where we are heading it is told to be an extraordinary place in the forest. I have come to hear that stray dogs and cats panic him and in order to avoid them he constantly crosses from one side to the other of the forest to another . . ."

"Oh, how come, Zuri?" asked Dominic curiously.

Speaking with a very subtle voice, and so muffled that it was hard to tell if Zuri was speaking at all.

'Zuri, could you speak louder.'

"I am feeling sleepy . . . anyway—John Mosaic whose family history has been followed from the Byzantine era is known to have a crystal clear face during sunrise. The three-eyed living being does not only carry the name mosaic but also signifies its piece within his body and surrounding. The ornamental figure is renowned to his shimmering masterpiece. His vibrant mosaic shaded body and emerald green chest signifies the open chakra having a great healing power that permits him to cure the spirit and their needs . . ."

'Wait a minute Zuri, is he some kind of beast. Three-eyed living being and crystal clear face during sunrise. What the f . . . why is everything becoming a fantasy!'

"Ashley, don't panic. Hear Zuri out," said Dominic in a flat voice.

'Still, Dominic, aren't you curious about this Mosaic man.'

"We all are and we got to be prepared about how exactly this man is or living being is. None of us know," spoke Dominic with a grating voice.

"Cool down, Ashley. I know you have been facing loads of things, but now is the time we stick together, so don't panic before anything even happens," voiced Charlie in an orotund tone.

Sigh, 'Fine guys. Go on Zuri. I was just surprised with an overwhelming detail.'

"It's okay. In the ancient world, mosaics were mostly used for floorings and boardwalks. The marble stones used were given a boon allowing them to easily break down and turn themselves into exceptional piece of art. Until one day an illuminating light appeared from a ladybug that was carved in the Byzantine Empire. The ladybug has been a long-time good luck myth bringing its magical essence to the marble piece of glasses that was known as mosaic," described Zuri in his silvery tone.

"Woh! Seriously!" interrupted Dominic.

Listening to Zuri's words calmly earlier and with all the mosaic details brought about a notion of entering a world of a magical feast in this real world I was living. How on earth was all this even possible?

Zuri added, "His best companion Barney Peacock pecks animal skin and sews various patchworks for John to justify his character and beliefs towards Mosaic. As we know, the two of them live eight hours away from the city's commercial area in this Rubik cube shaped home. What I heard was that each part of the house is made of a different colored mosaic with an artistic touch, from the walls to the ceiling to the furniture, lights and even the floor is all in mosaic inside. Referring to his three eyes, each eye has its own authority to destroy, protect and control. The first eye is sea blue representing sincerity, loyalty, trust, wisdom, and stability. The second eye is black in color associated with power, death, evil and strength portraying his dangerously mysterious character. The third eye is placed on his chest, red in color with black polka dot signify the ladybug a gift from his dynasty. The ladybug is known for its symbol of protection, happiness and love but because of the black dots, it does give him the power to turn anything upside down. The rest about him we got to see and learn now."

'I am overpowered with all these details. Are we making the right choice to go there? This was John's story, what about Barney's. Is she as phenomenal as John?' I asked quizzically.

"We have driven three hours now and this forest location is not so easy to find. We shouldn't head back as he can sense some people are going to be visiting. And a note to Ms Barney Peacock about us visiting had been sent already," said Darty in a husky voice.

"How do you know that, Darty?" asked Charlie.

"I don't know, I presume from what I have heard. He just knows when someone is coming near to visit. He senses everything."

"Freaky!" muttered Dominic.

'Oh well! What about the Peacock lady? How do you even know about her?' I asked.

"She is quite a woman. I mean-Peacock woman. I had come across her many years back when I used to go hunting. After I accidently shot her and did not realize she was not completely an animal, I panicked and begged for mercy. And she did give me a last chance to improve myself. From then on I have worshipped her and do visit her once in a while discreetly. Seldom anyone gets to see her. Hardly anyone knows she even exists," uttered Darty.

He added, "Barney Peacock carries this legacy from her father who was half human and half a bird. Barney's lower neck acts like a magnetic chakra that manages to control the negative energy evolving around. Her feathers acts like a glorious fan during sunset expressing her uniform division of eye feathers that protects her from any dust particles or cold spirit. In ancient history, Peacocks were considered symbols of nobility, protection, guidance and holiness. It is still believed that Barney once turned into peacock dives into spirituality attributes with an awakening vision that refines stray ghosts and their souls," described Darty in a guttural tone.

'That is surely amazing. She must be looking graceful and her power must be impressionable. I guess guys we are all in a mission. Both Barney and John are mystical characters,' I spoke cautiously.

"Yes, I hadn't any clue they even existed," mumbled Dominic with surprise.

The burst out of laughter echoed the car leaving a light hearted scenario. 'Is there anything more you know about her, Darty?'

"Hmm . . . oh yes, she is a mix of golden burnt yellow, dark blue and ruby red feathers. She has a human face and a body curved like a peacock and legs like a beautiful woman. Barney does not fail to disappoint Mosaic and has always been attracted to him. Her golden feathers are vibrant making her personality very lively. During sunset, sometimes her feathers turn orange creating an invisible magnetic attraction towards the universe.

When the color during the sunset changes, Barney's certain feathers have the ability to change color. Often Barney forms a crest made of her wavy feathers in a fan shaped fly into the trees to protect her or sometimes to indulge in a calm hibernation. But mostly one cannot see the fan flared feathers easily. She is simply beautiful, Ashley."

'I am more fascinated to meet Barney more than ever. She seems charismatic—peacock that can speak. How cool is that!'

"Your sense of humor, Ashley," teased Charlie.

The ride to the forest to meet John and Barney was getting adventurous and every detail about them was exceptional. The rising heart beat and keenness to explore every detail was getting thrilling.

The silence indicated pondering thoughts in everyone's mind. Another few hours to go and we would be able to watch the mystics of the ultimate healers.

## CHAPTER 24

# Meet and Greet with Ultimate Healers

"I need a beer!" said Dominic in his high pitched voice. The sudden laughter of the men and the continuous sound of them giggling like women didn't seem to end. Zuri snorted and it seemed as if there was a laughing gas in the car.

'What so funny Dominic? And a beer now!'

"It's all the overwhelming stories. I think we shall have a beer and slow down a little," blurted Dominic.

'Someone's worried now.'

Zuri turned around to see Dominic's facial expression. Charlie gave a heads up indicating that everything would be fine.

The journey to the forest was getting adventurous. Passing through grassy lands, seeing women walking pass through with clay pots, and men with cattle showed the morning routine by locals.

The sun's rays were shining brightly reflecting into the car window. Hearing Charlie snoring was disturbing my ears. The lack of sleep by everyone suggested a shot of espresso.

'I guess we should stop by a near café for some caffeine. The ambience is getting too sleepy and I need to wake up.'

"I would like that," uttered Dominic.

"That sounds good. I shall stop by a nearby neighborhood where some cafes are," expressed Darty.

We reached a neighborhood that was declining ethnic. We could spot apartment buildings and the two-flat wood frame house. One of the local cafes was in one of those two-story houses that needed repair. Paint flaked from the railing as we walked into the weaken front stairs of the house and a waiter came to take the order.

Charlie grinned. He was noticing my expression towards a local café that needed super maintenance. However, when the espresso was served in colorful shot glasses my disappointment towards the not so high-so ambience of the café subsided. Having being served scrambled eggs, banana crepe with toast was a treat to our famished tummies.

Chatting away, we all agreed to have savored some delicious brunch before embracing a new world of charm our way. We headed back to the car and drove into the beautiful greens.

To our surprise the road was not as bumpy as we thought it would be and we were there. The fragrance of the bushy plants, the sounds of the canary singing, and the crushing sound of rattling leaves were amazing.

I forgot to get my camera. The forest looked pretty with colorful flowers blooming. It was quite rare to see lesser wildlife. As we all started to walk deeper into the forest, forest lamps began to light up. Various designs of lamps were lit and the light blended well with an afternoon sky.

When Dominic, Charlie, Darty and Zuri reached an isolated area, the pebbles on the ground tested them. 'Zuri, you go first! You seem to know everything about him,' I spoke with fear.

When each person entered the walkway one needed to enter barefoot to scan their eyes through a mosaic glass machine while the pebbles on the floor recorded the pressure of the foot that tested their patience level, nervousness and level of cunningness.

"Oh Dominic, you can go first. I do know about him but I haven't met him before. Don't be a chicken," said Charlie and pushes him in front.

Dominic trips on his hand hurting one of the marshmallow pebbles, which makes all the pebbles, surround him and locks him on the spiral ground facing towards the painting of John Mosaic camouflaging with Barney Peacock. The painting was unusually beautiful that Dominic forgot that he was captured and kept glazing at the painting.

It was more like a painting of John who was covered into mosaic with peacock color elements while Barney was covered with mosaic shaped feathers to appreciate each other's beauty. While Dominic glazed into the picture, Ashley was worried about Dominic's wellbeing. She managed to walk on the pebbles patiently and successfully was granted the entrance to Mosaic's cubic mansion. Zuri, Darty, and Charlie calmly walked through the pebbles and were also granted to the house.

Dominic was released and thump—he was on the ground.

When Charlie and I entered the mansion, we were astonished by the vibrant reflection of ourselves around until we realized the entire house was made of mosaic glass. While looking around and scanning the entire area Zuri spotted a strange wall that was carved in a circular shape with a ladybug on the centre. He walked towards it and was just about to touch it when John appeared in front of him.

'How did you know we reached?' I asked curiously.

John's honeyed voice expressed, "You see the lady bug over here? That is my eye! How dare you try to poke my eye?"

Confused, Zuri said, "But I thought your third eye was on your chest according to Darty.

"Ahh I see . . . a lot has been looked up behind my back, but for your kind information all these lady bugs you see around represent my eye so I have the vision to see everywhere in my house and whereabouts of strangers," said John gruffly.

His eyes were blue in color and when one looked into his eyes they had the ability to get hallucinated in them by feeling pulled into the movement of the waves. Whenever he sensed a negative energy or a cold breeze brushing through his zinc solid bones his eyes turned coal black.

To having view that, it was freaky. "So Sir Mosaic, what does the painting outside your house depict?" asked Dominic politely.

"The oil painting is sketched with bright royal colors collected from animal pigment by Barney when she was on a hunt for cloth. I can sense the hungry minds," teased John.

John showed his side of sense of humor. Darty looked puzzled and uttered no word. His blah expression portrayed a shocking encounter.

'Thank you so much for allowing us to see you, Sir John. Your physical appearance brings no words since this is speechless. I never knew something . . . umm, oops . . . you existed. Where is Barney Peacock,' I spoke in a wobbly tone.

It was all so appealing yet scary.

With her penetrating voice, "I am right where I should be!" introduced Barney dramatically.

The colors within her were fortunately not produced by pigment but a natural gift given from nature. It was also the thin film interloping that took place in the barbules of her tail feathers that structured the magnificent shades and tints. This was one of the factors that made Barney gorgeous.

'Gorgeous!'

The stunned look on everyone's face was remarkable.

'Mr. Mosaic, I presume Ms. Barney Peacock has told you regarding our visit,' stated Darty politely after a long silence.

Zuri and Dominic began to get anxious as the house began to tremble as if an earthquake approached. Immediately the house rotated anti-clockwise slowly and the wall was now the floor.

'Did you perform some kind of magic? Everything is getting scarier,' I said dramatically.

"No magical retreat going on here. It is the pleasure of nature to entertain us today," exclaimed Barney with a wink.

Beneath the floor was a ten feet deep den structured with a spiral mosaic staircase where all Mosaic power seemed to be secured in each jar which could release each spirit with their problems. While we stepped down the stairs, the floor that was the ceiling was covered back and secured tightly. I spotted Dominic staring at a painting there, so patted him to get his attention.

The entire mansion was sparkly. Dominic brushed away a bee buzzing around his face.

In the same moment John flicks his nails through some pebbles and releases it in the air.

We wonder in astonishment trying to understand what was going to happen next. The entire sight of unexpected bewitchment one after the other was like an illusion.

Nothing happened! No extraordinary delusion was showed. In fact, the pebbles simply landed up on a purple crystal plate on a bookshelf next to his couch. His living room in the den was tiny, but air conditioned. The bright colored drapes were drawn and the intense sun's rays were welcomed in. We sat down on his couch and he popped open the beers. He had a beautiful fish aquarium and the colors of the fish were stunning in the bright room.

It was unusual to see the mosaic man have beers with the men. Settling back into his chair, John eyed Barney as she poured us fresh cups of coffee, adding lots of sugar and cream, whilst the men were clinking their beer mugs. Zuri leaned forward in his chair, his voice lowered dramatically, "When should we . . ."

"Not now! It's beer time, Zuri," said Barney interrupting Zuri.

"How did you know what I was going to ask Barney?"

"I just know. We shall have our chit-chat after some welcoming treat is being done. Then we shall go to solving your problems," said Barney in her appealing voice.

'Thank you again for having us here. Your humility is appreciated.'

Clearing his throat, "Let's talk about our humility when your problems are solved. For now enjoy the moment of coffee and beers," articulated John crisply.

No one dared to say anything further and coffee was sipped by order.

The caffeine intake was shooting my heart over a rocket speed. With all the chaos I was going through it was hard to stay calm and drink coffee.

There were minor difficulties and awkwardness, of course. But when John kept looking at me a couple of times, he started to ask me a few questions with concern. Perhaps he sniffed every fear cell in my body. I was acting too cool to feel anything.

"When did all this start, Ashley?" questioned John.

'Umm . . . when I started my journey away from Hawaii. When I reached Egypt I began to face peculiar situations. I was followed inside the Pyramids and saw images in Tanzania. When I got to the school, I had encountered numerous daunting events and could see moments of their death story. I could inhale their fear and despair. I have been having sleepless nights and when I started to understand slightly where I lived now, I had to surrender to their demands. And also when I had to face our principal and learning that she is a witch, I freaked out. Luckily Dominic believed in what I said. Phew!'

"I can see what you went through. So I believe you have the principal's photo and give me a brief scenario what you faced with the spirits," enquired John politely.

After having said what needed to be said about the six spirits and how many were left to embrace their new world. The entire picture of the problem was seen clearly.

Everyone was glaring at me with a shock having heard about how each spirit had died and how I got to see unusual tricks of each when they began to confide in me.

When tears begin to trickle down my face, Barney embraced me with her soft feathers. Her soft scent was pleasant diffusing of various fruits at that point.

Then, she moved on to the photo albums, framed pictures of her family and small porcelain gifts.

John and Barney assured me that everything would be solved and Principal Orchestra would have to be treated how she treated herself by sacrificing wild animals for her good luck charm.

Even though it was coming to a term end at school, strangely, the spirits never mentioned when they would leave. There was no sign of anything. What were they even up to was everyone's concern.

Sitting on the yellow couch was not bringing any positive notion at this point. The vibrant color was not rubbing its vibrancy on me. Glancing around the room lit with lemongrass candle fragrance was just getting me drowsy.

All of us expect John and Barney were wide awake. We were offered to nap in the underground basement for a few hours until rituals would be performed to bring a clear insight about Orchestra and her motives.

The small room given to us to rest our tired nervous system was quite cozy. There were exactly five individual soft white furry beds for us to sleep. There were no windows but various types of lamps were lit and peacock feathers were hung around the room.

As I lay on the bed, I felt hypnotized and got drowsier. I could not even sense where I was.

The entire ambience enveloped me in a new world where I didn't realize when I was clutched by a sound trance.

## CHAPTER 25

# Mosaic, Peacock & Orchestra

"My head is spinning, Ashley," blurted Dominic.
"Ashley—Ashley," called out Dominic repeatedly.

'Hmm, what happened Dominic,' I asked lying on my bed. I felt so good. The three of hours sleep was amazing.

"Oh, I think I am having a hangover. Something was in the beer. Doesn't usually happen that way . . ."

"Dominic, you are too weak for John's homemade beer," said Zuri teasingly.

"How did you know that," asked Dominic curiously.

"He mentioned it when he was offering. Try the homemade beer," uttered Zuri in his low voice.

It was clearly seen that everyone was feeling fresh except for Dominic. I couldn't even comprehend where the three hours went. And the soundness of the room was soothing. Awaking to soft peacock feathers and the reflection of lamps around was something different.

The option now was to wake up and get going with what we were here for. The sleep attack had to be fought against and knowing more about how we were to fight Orchestra was the key point here. Also knowing how John and Barney dealt with stuff like that would be interesting. They were indulged with complete magical powers and their intuition was simply commendable.

Well, everyone has their world of expertise. Having freshened up, I went up the spiral staircase into the other living room. To my surprise no one was there. The house mansion was empty and did not look like we were just here sometime ago.

I began looking around the place and saw the paintings again.

Whilst being engrossed into the paintings, I heard a hissing sound. As I turned around I saw a snake outside the window. A sudden jerk from behind me frightened me as John nudged me. He had camouflaged with the mosaic wall that I didn't notice him at all.

'Oh John, you scared the shit out of me. Why were you hiding?' I asked in a grating voice. Sigh.

"You were certainly frightened. I can sense your pulse. Alright, that was a bad try," laughed John.

'Not funny . . . umm . . . I am curious about the chandelier up there . . .' I said when Barney interrupted me. "Don't be curious, Ashley. Actually, above is the rooftop and that is the talking chandelier shaped into a golden bronze globe that has the power to emit light or darken the entire living area if John turns angry.

'What! Who—that's freaky, yet startling. A talking chandelier—what is it with you all. I am shocked with all these new facts. Since when have you been living here?'

"We are more than two hundred years old," answered John in his husky tone.

The physical appearance of John was appealing. Even though he was covered with tones of purple mosaic, he still had his charm with his wit and knowledge. The man who could probably be six foot four or five inches was not lanky. He could adjust his physique with the environment. If I was given a second choice, I would rather conduct and in-depth research on them.

"You know something about me, but you don't know about Barney's specialty . . ."

'No John, tell me.'

"Well, an angry Barney turns brick red and without giving a thought decides to kill the prey. Her feathers start flapping very hard and she starts singing, and shrieks angrily considering it as a bad omen. Barney has the power to bring the rain, known to approach a storm during her father's era when peacocks were sacrificed to bring rain. So you should be aware if she turns brick red. Just a warning!" described John.

The tease and the bickering between them seemed cute. They complimented each other so well.

Barney's unification between being a human was lesser and more overruled by the beauty of a peacock. Her hair was tied into a bun and small peacock feathers could be seen. The only difference was its silkiness and because it was wavy, it flapped every time she moved her head.

Time would tell and show how John's and Barney's anger and teamwork skills brings all the chaos I was facing to an end.

It was nearing dusk and the sun's rays were diminishing. After asking permission from John, I strolled nearby the home with Dominic and Zuri while the rest decided to stay back and rest. Barney joined us showing us around the home where colorful flowers bloomed open as she walked pass by. Butterflies followed her as she promenaded down the forest. The beauty of the wildlife budded fabricating the horror of some wild creatures. The tameness of each animal was sensational as they shared an instant connection with her.

Zuri pointed out toward the sunset and slowly we noticed a natural feast to everyone's eyes. During sunset certain feathers of Barney's turned orange creating a magnetic attraction.

The thrill to see something mystical like that was once in a lifetime. I could feel Dominic's hands slowly embracing my waist. The butterflies created a halo over our head as we saw above, symbolizing something passionate, until my bashful system retaliated. Looking into his eyes and in silence

I was asking him questions of what was actually happening between us.

The warmth in his eyes resembled a compassionate sunset showing various scenic colors diffused in the sky slowly leaving us to view the moonlight and shining stars. I could feel the affection from his side sinking into my system embracing me into a journey of a love palate filled with various sensations.

The short and instant gesture stirred up a new wave indicating something I was still unsure of. Dominic stepped back clearing his throat and looked away. It surely seemed as though he was trying to understand what he was going through, too.

For that moment both of us ignored what we were to feel and forgot what was supposed to be or not to be. Instead we noticed Barney's beautiful aura floating in a wave like pattern. Zuri looked edgy, "Barney, what do you eat for a living?"

She burst into laughter wondering where that came from, slowly holding her continuous flow of giggles she said, "Hmm . . . I feed on poisonous plants, insects and reptiles that crawl around my territory and enjoy barbequing them with great satisfaction. I do relish all sorts of fruits and nuts. Also, I believe that serpents are one of the animals that spirits transform themselves into so that's why I suck out the venom without any harm to my body. I then drain my blood out and serve it to the evil and spirits without harming myself that signifies immortality. This is needed to be done once in a while to quench the thirst of the evils by putting them in their right place."

"Wow! Thank you for sharing," said Zuri with a surprise.

"When you all leave from here, you would have a vague memory about all this. Subconsciously you all would remember what you saw and heard and don't worry you won't forget John and I, but some things are better to be discreet than in the open," said Barney politely and added, "It's time to start the rituals. John must have gotten the right stuff to feast Orchestra's revenge. Let's head back."

"Sure, let's go," said Dominic and he walked ahead of me without saying a word. The sudden silence between us was intruding my sane mind but I had to push that away to get completely engrossed for this new ritual to destroy Orchestra's intentions forever.

When we reached the mansion, each of us walked up the stairs to the attic. The attic was a small luxurious cozy living room where small crystal diamonds were hanging on the windows like curtains. The reflection of the lamps on the diamonds revealed various colors absorbed in white light. It looked so pretty.

Slowly as we stood, we were rising upwards as the marble ground was elevating gently and the glass ceiling opened making the entire room now an open terrace.

Viewing the stars and the moon from a distance was picturesque. John took some pieces of wood and lit them. The ambience was getting cooler and then all of us were feeling the chilled breeze around us. Our teeth chattered due to the growing cool breeze that signaled an opening of a ceremony to end evil intentions.

The bonfire looked classy as its flames rose and danced along with the direction of the wind.

John smiled as he confirmed with his gestures that he found all that was needed without any hunting.

Barney smiled. She placed a pair of deer skulls, hair from the elephant's tail, tiger's teeth, claws, dog bones, and various types of flowers, herbs, eucalyptus and mint leaves were placed on a wooden table.

The ritual started when John chanted something softly and Barney flapped her feathers to ignite the flame and that alerted Orchestra as she was provoked to arrive and surrender her evil powers for good.

The process was getting confusing as we didn't know what was going on, but because Darty had seen some voodoo practiced before he had briefed us with a slight hint of a possibility of an activity taking place.

Because Orchestra had been sending me death notes and threatened to kill me, it was imperative to cut a few strands of my hair and give it to John.

The entire scenario was beyond my understanding. I hadn't a clue what was going on. The blood dripping from the deer's skull was making me want to puke.

We were told to close our eyes so Barney and John could concentrate on our thought process, especially mine.

Slowly I could visualize the first day I met Principal Orchestra at her office and how she was too sweet to me, then at the luncheon where she offered me a glass of wine, then seeing the real her at the dining room when I went to get the mirror until how she transformed to a witch threatening me several times.

In sometime, the howling of wild dogs were heard.

I squinted so I saw the land rose around John in broken shadows, ragged height of a muddy ground, and bats were around us. I quickly shut my eyes as it was getting intense and I was ready to scream any moment. My chest began to haul excruciatingly. The fluctuation of various symptoms was swimming inside me.

I could feel some light shining on me vibrantly. As I opened my eyes I could see Orchestra's beaming green eyes. I was shocked to see her angry eyes standing there with revenge and hatred. As I tilted my head, the mirror was just standing in its comfortable position floating in the air.

When she moved positions, the mirror moved along with her. I looked around to see if I was the only person who could view this. But surprisingly everyone's eyes were on me in shock. Charlie, Darty, and Zuri moved away from me thinking Orchestra would simply chew them up with her scary eyes. Dominic sat there shivering in hysteria.

I couldn't move in shock. Even though it was quite chilly, I began get cold sweats.

John threw in the deer skulls, some flowers and strands of my hair into the flames. The crackling sound of the skulls caught Orchestra's attention.

As John sensed a negative energy, a cold breeze brushed through his zinc solid bones and his eyes turned coal black.

His mosaic body began to shift its mosaic pieces as he could be repelled by Orchestra's long years of practicing black magic. He stared at her, "Tell me! Since when have you been practicing and what is your motive? Tell me before you are destroyed completely."

Orchestra was appalled by John's fierce energy penetrating her system. She became rebellious and started to chant something in some weird language.

Barney threw in the tiger's teeth, claws and some herbs into the flames. With that Orchestra had gotten angrier and started to scream, "All because of you bitch! Ashley, you released all the souls. Even that twit—Roy, you granted him justice without my permission. Too easy of a solution you offered those malevolent souls. They should have never been released . . ."

"Shut up Orchestra! No one has to be detained by you. You are no one to decide about anyone's soul," said Barney hoarsely.

John continued to chant some mantras and threw the elephant's tail into the flames. Worse still, Orchestra was ignorant about Barney's secret. She was slowly being absorbed into Barney's hypnotism.

Barney's feather like hair started to flare whilst Orchestra's knotted hair and simian eyes alerted a battle.

I was having a problem to breathe as her spindly legs began to crawl towards me. Oh the elegant looking Orchestra was dark as sewage. All her pretentious moves were out in the open.

"You cannot take the school away from me. If I leave the school, the school leaves with me—I will destroy the entire school. All the creatures around the school will be waiting for only one sign and that's it—destroyed," shouted Orchestra arrogantly.

John sprinkled herbs, various flowers and mint leaves into the flames.

Orchestra began to get agitated as she could sense all her powers towards the animals she mentioned were slowly diminishing. Chanting loudly, Orchestra threw her ruby ring with a spear pointing out on John, but just in time Barney caught hold of it and threw it into the fire.

Orchestra fell on the ground and the mirror cracked into pieces. John sprinkled the remaining flowers and threw the eucalyptus leaves on Orchestra. A few that were stuck on his palm he sprinkled them into the flames.

Orchestra was panting louder and louder. Smoke had engulfed in the air. The fragrance of eucalyptus and mint was gasped in. A mist of being defeated had surrounded the environment as Orchestra's eyes were slowly changing back to hazel.

Orchestra's desperation to conquer had given up on her. It showed that all her tricks and powers were diminishing. To my surprise she wasn't turning into ash like they showed in movies nowadays. Her face became slightly wrinkled and her body dehydrated from the lack of warmth. She had polluted her entire system with revenge and captured souls for years.

Her age didn't depict her youth anymore. She looked as if she was suffering from some kind of disease that gently she was getting a paralytic attack. Her overestimation and overconfidence betrayed her over the powers of justice and goodness.

My body continued to quiver until it suddenly vanished. The desertion of her spell over me confirmed that this world was no more her territory of causing dismay and dark magic over people.

Orchestra's situation deteriorated but her ego and guilt did not leave her sight. There was no sense of repentance as she glared at me. Her strident voice attempted to fight her withdrawing powers as she uttered, "YOU MADE A BIG MISTAKE! Now your spirit friends will suffer . . . YOU . . ." and with that she was silent as she couldn't move her mouth no more. Her half body was paralyzed and her knotted hair slowly turned gray.

Barney plucked a feather from her hair and placed it on Orchestra's stomach. She began to chant something that sounded so harmonious and the mirror was shattered completely.

The cold darkness around us became pleasant. Orchestra was put on a wheel chair and Darty and Charlie drove her back to her home.

Dominic and I waited patiently as the atmosphere around us bloomed with shining stars and moonlight again. John's eyes were not black anymore.

Tears of joy trickled down and the tight hug by Barney soothed my emotional trauma.

That night the entire experience would never be forgotten by any of us.

John and Barney left Dominic and I at the rooftop as they decided to stroll around the forest to retain their powers towards righteousness.

Dominic sat beside me quietly as I continued my journey to detox with overflowing of tears trying to believe that it was surely coming to an end—justice was just around the corner.

The indictment of having friendly spirits around was just another moment to grasp as series of murky circumstances had never confirmed my acceptance of a friendly gesture towards them but a diplomatic acceptance of unfinished fulfillment.

The manifestation of serenity under the stars embraced my tired soul of fighting. The next scene was yet to encounter.

Sigh!

CHAPTER 26

# Liberation

Having woke up on Dominic's shoulder was comforting. The open rooftop had turned back into an indoor living room without us even realizing it. We were startled by birdsong echoing across the forest outside for a long time. The swelling orange sun was blazing the bright peachy wallpaper across from the living room.

Dominic looked at me with his expressive eyes, "How are you feeling now? Orchestra's gone Ash."

'I am much better Dominic. Thanks for asking. Yup—she's gone. Now there is another part to deal with. They must be waiting for me at school wondering where I went or they already know and would be disappointed. Am scared now! It just doesn't seem to get over.'

Hugging me tightly, "It will. It surely will. They had you around for a reason and now it's time to make that decision for them. Don't be scared. Am here and won't leave you."

'Thanks Dominic. You've been quite supportive all the way. We better get going downstairs and I need to speak to John and know what I should do next. Before any new ceremoney starts I got to meet the spirits atleast once and speak to them. I don't want a big backfire of any new dark magic again. I have had enough . . .'

"I know . . . don't worry. You go ahead I shall follow. I shall nap for another few minutes."

'Alright!'

As I walked towards the window, I opened them for some fresh air. I saw a Weaver flying over a glass sharp wall and dropped beside its shadow under a mango tree, stalking anxious insects. Under the broken birdhouse a cat played with a nibble of leftover meat. Shadows shrivel in bright coyness against the Rubik cube house.

Oh the beauty of this place was hard to find. I don't even remember staying at a forest ever. The bird's chirpiness, squirrels twirling movements, hissing of snakes, and many other nature's assets were enjoying their habitat.

Stretching away, I walked down the stairs to find John. Looking around the home, I entered the cozy kitchen. It was so cute to see the chimney inside a Rubik home. The interior of the kitchen was colorful and utensils matched the colorful mosaic around. Spotting Barney slurping on some worms with her hot cup of coffee made me feel disgusted. Who has worms with coffee? Obviously—Barney does. EEuuu!

As she saw me, she kept the worms away and chewed on some berries. "So—want some breakfast? You're quite hungry."

'Yup, I am. Anything to eat—no worms, please.'

Smiling, "Worms are delicious! But you can have the berries, walnuts, apricots, some fruits, and boiled eggs with chocolate syrup. Oh you should sprinkle the mango and cream custard on the nuts and fruits. We don't have much variety that suits your taste buds. John and I usually eat this and of course if he is quite in his mood he would eat an eagle for lunch."

'Fruits, nuts, eggs with chocolate syrup! Umm . . . Eagle for lunch—I would be on a diet then if I had to eat an eagle.'

"John doesn't like sharing his eagle, so don't worry about that. Help yourself with coffee, it's kept right there and the rest for your appetite is placed on the counter behind you. I shall go look for John."

Having trying what Barney said about chocolate syrup over my fruits, nuts, and eggs, I took a bite. Oh my, it was so delicious. I could always do with another bowl. The mango and cream custard was so creamy and mouthwatering. Also, spotting some baked potatoes with some herbs was breakfast complete.

I wonder when Dominic wakes up; he would eat the entire thing.

I took my serving and sat outside on the sofa. As I ate a few bites, I could hear some growling sound. Surveying the room quickly I saw nothing. Now it was getting obnoxious. I couldn't eat in peace. The sound was getting louder.

I continued to eat trying to ignore the sound, and then I heard a burping sound. The sound was loud and clear and came from behind me. Standing up quickly in shock, I turn around, John was chewing. I could only see his face as his body was blended with the wall.

'What are you doing? Are you trying to kill me by your burp? What are you eating anyway?'

"Who dies with a burp! Don't be silly and continue eating. I was just finishing my breakfast . . . care to taste an eagle's head."

'Sick—hell no! Barney mentioned that would be your lunch.'

"Oh, well I told her I changed my mind. For lunch I might eat you—you smell delicious . . . come on, before you freak out—I might eat what you are eating. I am easy! So, what's your next plan?"

'I was going to ask you that. I mean about the next plan. About the spirits I was telling you before, I believe it's time for them to leave but they haven't. Before we start any rituals I would like to meet the four of them . . .'

"Wait a minute! You know that's risky, right? Spirits are not allowed here and you have to travel eight hours away. So you would risk driving back and forth for them? Also, if they sense something they could revolt against you . . ."

'Seriously, you think they would do that when I have helped them in many ways, John. Can you sense something? Please tell me. I need to be aware. Can we call them here?'

"Nops, they can't come here! I guess the journey of any spirit ends from the beginning of the forest. We have protected it that way and only when things got to end they would arrive here. But we shouldn't underestimate the dynamism of desires. They can be intense developing a strong power of vengeance, Ashley. Now you got to decide whether you want to visit them or come back again."

'Umm . . . I would like to go back and meet them once. I believe I owe them a last conversation without telling them what would happen next. I am sure they would be happy to leave if I asked them they were ready to do so.'

"You really think so they would be so happy to leave. They haven't even told you whether they want to any time soon. Before you leave, take this purple crystal with you. If you are attacked by them, this crystal would alert me. And it would change its color to black alerting you to rush back into the forest, so you can come here. We don't have much time, if you leave, you must very now."

'Now John, but I just finished breakfast . . .'

"No drama, just leave now. Tell Dominic to get ready quick. Darty should be back by the time you guys are ready. You're sure about this?"

'Yes! Why so? Sarah, Judy, Viera, and Edward would be happy to see me.'

"Alright Ashley! Go get ready then," ordered John.

John's assertiveness showed that either he was up to something or there was something he wasn't telling me. But I didn't want to crack my head with all those assumptions.

I went to the room and untied my hair. Brushing my hair so it would be untangled, I then took my clothes and went to take a shower.

My eyes closed, cold water cascading down over my body, I realized I forgot to wake up Dominic. Goodness, he has been sleeping like a log.

Well I had no choice, but enjoying the cold water. Carefully massaging my scalp with lavender shampoo I heard the shuffle of the shower curtain and felt the presence of someone in the bathroom. "Good morning," said Dominic in a husky voice.

'WTF . . . what you doing here?' I said loudly.

"Next time lock the door. I did open it slowly and noticed no one there, so I really needed to pee so got in hearing you hum softly."

'Still! You should not be here!'

"Why, shouldn't I be here . . . I need to pee and I am not intruding in your shower . . . unless you want me . . ."

'Oh shut up! Please leave, now I got to hear you pee.'

"Deal with it. I should be done soon. Ashley, I can feel you being nervous and you would still be cute," said Dominic with a tease.

He was right, I was so freaking nervous. I turned so my back would be facing the shower curtain. I hoped in silence he wouldn't do anything silly, but—SHIT—he embraced me gently from outside the curtain sending unwanted shivers. I couldn't imagine what he was up to. He laughed out loud and left the bathroom quickly.

For a few seconds, I was out of breath and it surely confirmed that he was driving me nuts. I quickly rinsed my hair and rushed out.

Having gotten ready, I wore my sunglasses and went downstairs waiting for Dominic. But he was still having his breakfast. Seeing him chatting with Barney, I sat on the other side of the room and looked outside the window.

Dominic knew I was there, and to my surprise when he was going upstairs he tapped my shoulders. When I turned around, he removed my sunglasses. "You don't have to be that shy with me. Nothing happened," he winked and went upstairs.

I could feel the heat all over my body knowing I must be blushing like strawberries. And hearing a chirping sound I glanced into Barney's direction noticing she saw everything as she smiled, "You two surely have it going on—HEATY!" She giggled.

'Oh Please! Barney. Dominic is a big flirt and . . .'

"He is a flirt—he likes you—maybe a lot! I can see that. Well that's not what we are here for. So you guys better get going, Darty is here. He is sitting by the waterfall."

'I have no comments, Barney. Okay, since he is here already, I shall wait at the waterfall too. The scenic view shouldn't be missed. Tell Dominic, we would . . .'

"I know, I will tell him you guys are waiting there."

'It's amazing how you can tell or sense anything one has to say. About Dominic, please don't say anything to him. I know I can't hide it from you, but truly don't need any romance now.'

"You don't need romance now—save it for celebration when you have been set free. Celebrate it later; acknowledge it later when the time is right. And you both would know it's time."

'You really think that! You really think all this would be over and the spirits would leave easily. They are very stubborn . . .'

"They are stubborn and we are healers! We heal and everything is wiped out. Go to the waterfall and don't think too much."

I obeyed her like a little baby girl with a load of Dominic's thoughts in my mind. As I saw the rush of waters gushing down the stream, my load of notions subsided. I sat down on one of the rocks gazing at the beautiful flow of waters.

"HEY WE CAN LEAVE NOW!" screamed Dominic from a few meters away.

I signaled Darty by waving my hand that we could leave to the school. As we walked towards the exit of the forest, we had passed many trees that left a sweet, clean fragrance of freshness—as one was inhaling the purest oxygen without any contamination.

I couldn't look into Dominic's eyes and focused on my path towards the parked car.

As Darty got into the car, the huge tree fell on the car getting him stuck inside. He couldn't move or even open the door easily.

As I turned around Dominic was captured by a net pulling him upward. I freaked out and gulped down in horror.

Everything was fine a few minutes ago. What just happened, I wondered curiously. The sweet fresh fragrance was contaminated with vengeance when I saw Edward. He was sitting on top of the car.

When I turned around, Sarah and Viera were standing below Dominic. I was trembling, so I turned in front again and saw Judy's red eyes in resentment.

"Ashley! You betrayed all of us," said Judy in anger.

'No, I didn't. I was just going to drive to school to see you guys . . .'

"NO! YOU'RE LYING. YOU LEFT WITHOUT SAYING ANYTHING TO GET RID OF US WITHOUT OUR CONSENT," spoke Sarah in a hoarse voice.

'Umm . . . what do you mean without your consent, Sarah. Don't you guys have any intention to leave? School semester ends and you . . .'

"It's up to us when we want to leave, Ashley!" interrupted Viera rudely.

I had so much to say and now I was blank. Darty was trying to get out of the car but couldn't as Edward locked all the doors. His pressure on the car was so strong that the metal ceiling was slowly denting.

When I looked at Dominic, he was shocked and I could see his worried eyes. I could not imagine I was trapped exactly out of the forest. John had asked me a several times and warned me in some way—But!

"Don't think too much! You are not set free until we decide to leave you or the school. We have no intention of leaving anytime soon," screamed Edward.

Edward's eyes were no more innocent but awful as he sneered.

Lightning had strike in a pleasant summer weather. It began thundering. Everything was getting confusing and I couldn't think straight with the spirits fast movement.

Sarah had pulled my hair and pushed me hard toward the bark of the tree. The pressure was strong that I lost balance and banged my head hard. I fell backward and very quickly I was floating in the air rotating in circles getting me giddy and faint.

I was then thrown on the ground harshly that I puked and felt very low in energy. My eyes were shut but I could hear John's words—hold the crystal in your hand and I shall get the signal.

Very wearily I managed to get out the purple crystal and saw it change its color to black. The crystal melted on my palm and that got me alerted what I was supposed to do.

There was no way any of us to escape. The four desperate spirits didn't give me a chance to say anything but attacked me brutally. This surely proved that they probably didn't have any goodness left.

Until I was feeding them their desire they were calm. After one doubt I was attacked.

Judy dragged me from my hair high up in the air. I was held by Edward and Sarah for balance.

I was then floating toward the direction of the school. As we probably went a few hundred meters ahead, to my surprise I saw peacock feathers glowing in appearance. We were blocked with thousands of feathers in the air.

Judy and Edward threw me over the branches of a tree. Fortunately, I caught the balance and held the branches tightly and slowly managed to jump down on the corner of the road.

When I looked up, Barney had appeared and had captured the spirits with her feathers.

Barney's admirable and perfect timing saved me from getting killed by them. I couldn't stand properly, so sat down by the road.

Eyes glistened from tree hollows. The wind yowled between deformed trunks, transmitting the oddly whiff of wood decay.

The stinky smell around me provoked me to stand up and start walking to the direction of the forest. The pungent odor of rotted bodies was getting clearer, as I recognized the smell when Edward and Judy were narrating their story to me.

After having walked for a couple of minutes, I inhaled a minty smell and continued on delighting in the fragrance sliding through the leaves feeling protected by John.

John's and Barney's intuition was commendable and nature's gift.

I couldn't see Darty or Dominic anywhere.

My exhausted body needed water dreadfully. The sound of squirrels chattering, rustle of animals rooting in underbrush, and scrabbling of lizards on tree bark were not as scary as the sudden attack by the spirits. I was still in shock. I couldn't believe whatsoever and they were cable of doing that to me when I was only going to help them. Now, I was sure they had to leave by hook or crook.

No mercy or sympathy was to be proffered to the ungrateful spirits. It was time for them to LEAVE!

I was panting away . . .

# CHAPTER 27

# Fête

I could hear wind chimes from a distance knowing I was probably near. Everything felt so far because I was so tired.

From behind, Dominic hugs me tightly and as I turn around he kisses my lips. I hug him tightly and tears trickle down my face as I feel protected and normal again.

I shudder and step back. He held my hand, "I am so relieved you are okay. There is no need to step back. I know you feel the same way, Ashley. I won't hurt you, love.

Come, let's go and beat the shit out of these spirits."

I couldn't stop crying. I was pulled in his arms and I continued to weep like a baby. Resting my head on his chest for sometime was the greatest comfort of all times. I felt alive again.

As I looked up, 'Dominic, you can't beat the shit out of the spirits, John and Barney will. I like your sense of humor even at the moment.'

Patting my back, we enter the Rubik mansion, we head to the rooftop and see that Sarah, Judy, Viera and Edward are tightly clasped by Barney's feathers. The strength of the feathers could easily sustain the pressure of restless movements by the spirits.

"Leave us you crazy bird!" shouted Judy.

"YES—LEAVE US—OR ELSE!" yelled Edward.

Darty was sitting in the corner of the room to view the entire ritual and struggle of the spirits.

'I tried to help you. You guys are ungrateful. I was coming to see you, but you attacked me. You didn't even hear me out. You all are ungrateful—Roy and Thomas were grateful. You guys need to go and STOP CREATING A CHAOS,' I yelled out of frustration.

"Step back, Ashley," ordered John.

"Your life will be a graveyard you wait and watch ASHLEY!" exclaimed Sarah.

Within that moment, John splashed snake blood on them. The spirits began to get more restless and their emotions were clashing with retaliation. One could see that every molecule they had in their spirit body was denying the fact that they could still live longer on the Earth's plain to haunt people for their never lasting quench of desire.

Their desire was simple yet a poison to anyone's wellbeing. Especially mine!

Dominic caught hold of my hand and we stepped backwards. For me this entire scenario was nothing like watching *Harry Potter, The Mummy, The Lord of the Rings* or even *The Chronicles of Narnia*. It was purely real and it only left goosebumps when one could see a battle between the dead and the gifted healers.

When snake blood was splashed on the spirits, I thought I would faint, but no I didn't. In fact, when John handed me the remaining snake blood, I splashed it on them seeing them drip and how their physical body was soon fading.

Then a crow flew into the rooftop region. Crow strained his wings and flew around Sarah, Judy, Edward, and Viera. Suddenly, the daylight world burst upon them with all its grandeur and luminosity. The eternal shades of color surrounding them made the crow gape intensely. He then flapped down and rested himself in the middle of the four spirits. Above him, the sky was blue, the clouds feathery and white.

The view could be seen clearly making it like an artistic gift of freedom. With that, nature was absorbing the negativity from the spirits as a flow of reddish brown flakes from all were flowing into the fluffy clouds slowly turning it gray.

Once the clouds turned gray, the crow flew away and rested on a branch of tree nearby.

It started to get warm as Barney lit the bonfire. The bonfire this time was bigger and John threw eleven glass cups into it. The crackling sound, melting of glass resulted in an odd and musty smell. The putrid odor diffused making all of us hard to breath. Dominic, Darty and I covered our faces with a thick napkin to not get suffocated.

The crow flew back dropping a crystal ball into the flames. It smashed to smithereens upon the ground, absolving the sunshine so that it detonated up and out, enlightening every dark place and chasing away every dark shadow. The sky grew bright and turned turquoise. The hills took on the luminosity and form. Then snow started falling as ice sparkled so vibrantly that the bonfire did not extinguish but was surrounded by drizzling snow.

The magnificent beauty of the drizzling snow surrounding the bonfire was picturesque. The combination of two weathers brought about a soothing feeling developing a revolt against the nature of the spirits as they were trying eagerly to be set free.

Edward and Judy were screaming. They began to cry so loud that bullet shots were heard as if they were losing their lives. I then remembered the way they were killed by officials to end many poachers lives.

Puzzled and terrified, Judy began getting weak by collapsing on the ground. The heat she emitted from her body was intense. Beside her, Edward was struggling to breathe. "HELP US!" they cried in pain.

The realization of the truth reflected on them recognizing that they were meant to die and never come back. They were to ascend and acknowledge a new world living the highest of good and light.

Their continuous tears of despair slowly subsided when Judy said, "I can feel it. It's time to go. Sorry . . . we should go . . ." and she gradually faded away like dust into the air.

As I glanced toward Darty, he was weeping. It seemed that he could feel their pain. Edward couldn't manage to say anything but, "Sorry . . . have a good life, Ashley."

As Edward faded away like Judy. Sarah and Viera grew angrier. They could not face the fact they had to leave. They didn't want to surrender.

I had my last chance to say something that would perhaps make a difference in their thoughts, only if they wanted to listen.

'Sarah and Viera, don't torture yourself. And simply surrender. This would . . .'

"Shut up Ashley! Because of you, Judy and Edward are gone and they faced shit," yelled Viera in anger.

Before Sarah could say anything, John sprinkled some herbs, incense sticks, and rose petals into the bonfire.

The reaction it brought to Judy and Sarah was unbelievable.

They began to weep and begged for mercy. Judy yelled in agony.

The fragrance of rose petals fused within their rebellious nature bringing upon passion and repentance.

Dominic left my hand and moved to sit in the corner. He needed a moment to be alone. I sat there putting down my napkin to inhale the aroma of rose everywhere.

Barney gave me a few petals and told me to blow it towards the direction of them. As I followed instructions, Sarah and Judy said together, "Thank you . . . sorry . . ."

They slowly evaporated like mist. The mist was engulfed with dark red smoke emitting sparkling dusts of rose petals.

Like that the four spirits left leaving bitter sweet memories.

My journey started in Hawaii and ended in a rooftop releasing spirits in a forest. Everything had come to an end which left me with tears of joy.

The surprise entry of John and Barney in my life brought about a miracle. A magic indeed!

At dusk, when Barney cooked John's special eagle, for a moment I was distracted as I could see the love she had for him. Although they were not romantic, their wit and compassion for each other was deep and nothing could separate them. Every hurdle was never a hurdle and there was a balance of thoughts and actions between the two ultimate healers. Their positivity and determination taught me something new. And that was love—love again—love accepting Dominic.

John opened a few bottles of beers and this time we all drank with glory.

Barney's untied long silky and feathery hair carpeted the ground. John quietly came over and sat over her hair and kissed her cheek.

Darty smiled.

When Barney blinked, the entire mansion was lit with colored candles and incense sticks at certain corners.

The calming affect it brought healed everyone's troubled mind. John and Barney kept away their beer bottles and tranquilly chanted something that we could hardly remember what we saw. It seemed like it happened a long time ago.

The warmth and ambience they brought about was something I would never forget in this lifetime.

Our chit-chat, snack time was over after savoring fruits, sautéed potatoes and pumpkin, avocado salad, and grilled fish with herbs.

John and Barney went for a stroll in the forest. As we followed them, we lost our way, so we stopped to look at the shining stars shining over various fruit trees and flowers.

After spending some time manifesting the beauty, we were back into the guest room and no one said a word. Sleep had invaded our souls deliberately and the night had passed by with pride.

The clinking of wind chimes woke us up the next day.

After wrapping myself in the thickest towel, I pat my skin dry. Small drops of water still dripped from my hair, causing tiny rivers down my spine as I begin to wear my clothes.

We had our morning coffee and were all ready to head back to our labor of love. We were running out of time and Darty was already muttering like an old man.

This time there would be no spirits—and Principal Orchestra's story would bring a new twist to a new job placement of a principal. The art of earning a living couldn't be forgotten as we were not granted any boon by a genie.

The ambience of the entire mansion was captivating that I wished I could live a simple life and stay with John and Barney under the shelter of living rightly and with passion. They had their goals of their existence and we had ours. It was time for the goodbyes and we were ready to leave.

John and Barney had invited us back for tea after a few weeks when everything had settled at school. Their warm gesture was comforting.

We were all set to go, Dominic sat in the front accompanying Darty. Our ride continued for hours recalling all that happened and how grateful we were.

Dominic kept turning behind occasionally smiling at me. I knew it, I could tell, he was so happy like he had never gone through a breakup recently. So did I feel the same.

I would surely share this love story with Edwin when I would call him in a few days as it was his birthday.

Some things are just crazy enough to believe that happiness can come back in one's life—this time even better—thrilling—compassion—worth every emotion.

We went back to the café we had stopped by earlier when we were heading to meet John and Barney. The aroma of the fresh coffee late evening was refreshing and a fuel to a tired soul.

When the souls were energized we took off back to school.

Having passed calm fields, and then entering the fine architecture of the school got us to wonder that how could anything ever be wrong here. But the hallucination and experience I went through was fearful and something I wanted to forget like a bad nightmare.

I know my best counselor would be Dominic. At this point of time, being so tired, I simply entered my nest leaving Dominic behind. He was kind enough to give me my space to foster some energy for the next day of class.

Having done all the routine activities, I settled on my soft bed. For a change, it seemed like it had been weeks.

All the frightful incidents had gotten me to forget any good moment could arrive until Dominic hugged and kissed me. Oh that feeling, butterflies.

Now it was the continuation of a few weeks of classes and a new semester to begin after two months. It was time to visit Hawaii and share my new trail of experiences. With these notions, god knows when I dozed off.

The next morning, after a shower and a heavy breakfast at the cafeteria, I met Charlie. He mentioned that Orchestra had been shifted to an old wooden house and he volunteered to provide her food until she lived.

'Charlie, that's really kind of you to help Orchestra out.'

"Well, I thought of doing some good for her. Hopefully she realizes what she aimed for was not right. But evil will always be evil. Oh, have you heard, about the new placement for principal," said Charlie calmly.

'Yes, I just did. I hope this time it's a good one—someone who has no witchcraft experience. Also, the sudden outbreak of Orchestra's sickness has surprised everyone.'

"Yes, it has. Goodness! No one knows what her intentions were. Anyway, I better get going back to finishing my tasks. You have a good and normal day now onwards," spoke Charlie with a smirk.

'Thanks, I am looking forward to a normal day without any intruders.'

Sometimes, fatal moments don't bring about any mercy or even any empathy. It is always better to let go and the process to forget an incident needs time—sometimes a lot of time.

Having getting back to routine, it was nice to have a good class where no supernatural act was performed. My heart didn't skip a beat with fear.

Later that afternoon, sounds of drums, flute, and violin were heard being played in the drama room. The melodious collaboration of instruments was harmonious. The sound of every beat and note developed a right vibration to celebrate a new beginning.

I paced along the beat and stopped at the field when I saw parti-colored balls of blaze disperse in all directions and then burst as they plunged back to earth. Wave after wave of luminescent vehemence jazzed across the grassy field. That distracted me, so I walked towards a groups of students to see what they were doing.

After having asking around, they were using left over firecrackers so they could buy new ones for Christmas. Being under the supervision of Dominic, I knew where their naughty thoughts came from.

Dominic stood there smiling and I went with the flow. Finally a rocket was lit and it gracefully shot up towards the bright sky leaving the sound of freedom.

The semblance of a fun character indicated a stroll towards the church.

For a change, seeing the church bell silent was peaceful. As I walked past it, I could see the church bell rope getting longer as I paced ahead.

I turned around wondering what was going on. The rope became shorter and shorter dangling sideways. The church bell began to ring without anyone's support.

Now my heart skipped a bit.

Oh no!

# ACKNOWLEDGEMENTS

Marvelous is the mind and motivation is geared through various people. I would like to thank my family for their progressive support towards living life wholeheartedly.

I appreciate and express gratitude towards Partridge Singapore to be encouraging at every step of this publication. All my friends have always been effortlessly encouraging and excited to see my labor of love. There has been loads of support and cheering from many people who have been part of my journey of life. I am grateful for the love, wit, naughty comments and kindness.

My true inspiration and enthusiasm also came from the mind of the youth—students. They have always brought about a better day to my life. Special appreciation goes to my illustrators—Pangnaphaphat Rukspollmuang (Tina), Milan Khemlani, and Jupe Manisa Churesigaew for their creative talent. (Yuppie!)

Last but not the least, I thank the Almighty God, my Master, and the beautiful dream of the stars and moon smiling at me. Without the embrace of positivity and gratitude from the universe this would not have been completed on desired time.

Thank you everyone. I shall dive into a new set of notions and pen down a new interesting story. Wink! Wink!

Printed in the United States
By Bookmasters